Walter Hamilton

A lyttel Parcell of Poems and Parodyes

in Prayse of Tobacco, Contayning divers Conceited Ballades, and Pithie Sayinges

Walter Hamilton

A lyttel Parcell of Poems and Parodyes
 in Prayse of Tobacco, Contayning divers Conceited Ballades, and Pithie Sayinges

ISBN/EAN: 9783744782241

Printed in Europe, USA, Canada, Australia, Japan

Cover: Foto ©Andreas Hilbeck / pixelio.de

More available books at **www.hansebooks.com**

An Odd Volume for Smokers.

A LYTTEL PARCELL OF

POEMS AND PARODYES

IN PRAYSE OF

TOBACCO,

contayning divers conceited Ballades, and pithie sayinges,

All newly collected and emprinted, by

WALTER HAMILTON,

Fellow of the Royal Geographical, and Royal Historical Societies.
Author of "The Poets Laureate of England," "A History of National
Anthems and Patriotic Songs," "A Memoir of George Cruikshank."
"The Æsthetic Movement in England."
Editor of Hamilton's "*Collection of Parodies.*"

—✧✧✧—

" *Let those smoke now—who never smoked before,*
And those who always smoked—now smoke the more."

—✧✧✧—

London.
REEVES & TURNER, 196, Strand, W.C.

MDCCCLXXXIX.

POEMS AND PARODYES IN PRAYSE OF

TOBACCO.

501 *Copies of this Collection have been printed on hand-made Paper, of which 151 are Presentation Copies, and 350 are for Sale.*

ACROSTIC.

TO thee, blest weed, whose sovereign wiles,
O'er cankered care bring radiant smiles,
Best gift of Love to mortals given!
At once the bud and bliss of Heaven!
Crownless are kings uncrowned by thee;
Content the serf in thy sweet liberty
O charm of life! O foe to misery!

J. H.

ON the first Friday in December, 1888, a paper entitled "SONGS IN PRAISE OF TOBACCO" was read before "Ye Sette of Odd Volumes" in Willis's Rooms, King Street, St. James's; His Oddship, T. C. Venables, Esq., in the chair.

According to the usual practice of the Sette that paper should have been printed for private circulation amongst the members only, unfortunately it was impossible to comply with that custom.

The paper contained many parodies relating to smoking, it was imperative that these should be included in my COLLECTION OF PARODIES, and it would have been contrary to the strict O.V. etiquette to have reprinted any matter which had once been included in the reports of their proceedings. Besides which the poems were so numerous that they could not have been contained in a brochure of the thickness of the usual O.V. publications. The whole collection has therefore been re-arranged, and in addition to the Parodies (which have already appeared in print) all the best poetical praises of Tobacco are here gathered in one sweet-smelling bouquet, which is dedicated, with all respect and esteem, to those congenial spirits, and true lovers of the Indian Weed, the SETTE OF ODD VOLUMES,

by their grateful Friend,

and Brother,

The Parodist.

Contents.

𝔄 𝔏𝔶𝔱𝔱𝔢𝔩 𝔓𝔞𝔯𝔠𝔢𝔩𝔩 𝔬𝔣 𝔓𝔬𝔢𝔪𝔰 𝔞𝔫𝔡 𝔓𝔞𝔯𝔬𝔡𝔶𝔢𝔰 𝔦𝔫 𝔓𝔯𝔞𝔶𝔰𝔢 𝔬𝔣 𝔗𝔬𝔟𝔞𝔠𝔠𝔬.

LIGHTING-UP.

IT is almost universally admitted that the primeval smokers of the world were the natives (so-called *Indians*) of North America, who had been smokers for ages before the discovery of their country by the Spaniards, and who looked upon Tobacco with superstitious awe as a special gift sent by the Great Spirit for their delectation.

The custom of smoking was moreover widespread, for wherever the early explorers travelled on the Western Hemisphere the tribes with whom they came in contact were smokers, and from that date to the present time the votaries of the weed have been ever on the increase.

TOBACCO (*Nicotiana tabacum*) is said to derive its name from Tabacco, a province of Yucatan; other authorities trace it to the isle of Tobago, in the West Indies; whilst some say it comes from Tobasco in the Gulf of Florida. Tobacco was known in San Domingo in 1492, and was used freely by the Spaniards in Yucatan as early as 1520, but the exact date of its introduction into England cannot be definitely fixed.

It was either first brought over by Sir John Hawkins in 1565 or by Sir Walter Raleigh and Sir Francis Drake in 1586. Thus we know with tolerable certainty that smoking in England has lasted a little more than three centuries, and that notwithstanding the edicts of kings, the bulls of popes, the most stringent Acts of Parliament, the repressive " Smoking Prohibited " of dictatorial Railway Directors the solemn warnings of doctors, the anathemas of the Priesthood, and the frowns of the Ladies, the practise of smoking has been ever on the increase, and is now far more largely indulged in by high and low, rich and poor, than it has ever been.

In compiling the following pages much assistance has been derived from F. W. Fairholt's *Tobacco, its History and Associations*; from *Cope's Tobacco Plant*, published by Messrs. Cope Brothers and Co., Limited, Liverpool; from Mr. P. H. Davis; and from Mr. Caton, the obliging editor of *Tobacco*, to whom I am also indebted for the loan of some of the humorous illustrations which originally appeared in *Tobacco Jokes for Smoking Folks*.

The late Mr. William Bragge, of Sheffield, was a most persevering collector of antiquities, books, and other articles relating to the history of Tobacco, and relics connected with smoking.

Mr. Bragge's work, *Bibliotheca Nicotiana*, a catalogue of books about Tobacco, although issued some years ago, is still the standard book of reference on this subject.

His library, which contained nearly the whole literature of Tobacco, was sold in London by Messrs. Sotheby, Wilkinson and Hodge in April, 1882, and about the same time the following verses appeared in *Punch* :—

PIPES OF ALL PEOPLES.

Pipes of all peoples! Here's a strange collection,
  Made by one Bragge, the pipes of every clime,

Arranged in cases offered for inspection
   To all the *virtuosi* of our time.
Others have gathered china, insects, pictures
   Of modern men or masters old and ripe ;
Here is a man who, scorning sneers or strictures,
   Has gathered, to astonish us—the Pipe.

Here are queer pipes from Burmah and from Java,
   From Turkey, Russia, and from far Japan,
Some made of wood, of ivory, and lava,
   Some that belonged to pre-historic Man.
From Mexico come pipes of terra-cotta,
   That hapless MAXIMILIAN kept awhile,
And 'mid the whole Collection there is not a
   Pipe that's more strange than this from near the Nile.

Then come the pipes wrought skilfully of metal
   The Red Man's calumet, or pipe of peace,
Pipes that were smoked o'er many a camp-fire kettle,
   And others hailing from the hills of Greece.
Pipes made of reed from Amazonian valley,
   With meerschaums from Vienna of to-day ;
Pipes that would grace the huge mouth of "Aunt Sally,"
   The welcome cutty formed of humble clay.

All these and many more are here before us,
   That once in smokers' mouths were in full blast.
Light up cigars and pipes, and cry in chorus,
   "We'll smoke as men have smoked in ages past."
Havannahs whisper, "Try us and consume us."
   Tobacco tempts in variegated stripes.
Then "*Gloria*," we echo, "*Mundi fumus*,"
   And here's to BRAGGE and all his wondrous pipes !

POEMS IN PRAISE OF TOBACCO.

In the following pages the poems are thus arranged—on Tobacco generally, on the Pipe, Cigar, and Cigarette, and on Snuff. No poets have been found, however, to sing the praise of chewing Tobacco, a very old form of enjoying the weed. This habit is now principally confined to sailors, soldiers, policemen, and others whose duties compel them to remain in solitude for many hours at a stretch without the solace of a pipe. The following amusing letter shows the importance a sailor attaches to his Quid :—

GRAVESEND, March 24, 1813.

Dear Brother Tom ;
    This comes hopein to find you in good health as it leaves me safe anckor'd here yesterday at 4 P.M. arter a pleasant voyage tolerable short and a few squalls.—Dear Tom—hopes to find poor old father stout, and am quite out of pig-tail.—Sights of pig-tail at Gravesend, but unfortinly not fit for a dog to chor.
    Dear Tom, Captain's boy will bring you this, and put pig-tail in his pocket when bort. Best in London at the Black Boy in 7 diles, where go acks for best pig-tail—pound a pig-tail will do, and am short of shirts. Dear Tom, as for shirts ony took 2 whereof one is quite wored out and tuther most, but don't forget the pig-tail, as I aint had a quid to chor never since Thursday. Dear Tom, as for shirts, your size will do, only longer. I liks um long—get one at present,

best at Tower-hill, and cheap, but be particler to go to 7 diles for the pig-tail at the Black Boy, and Dear Tom, acks for pound best pig-tail, and let it be good.

Captain's boy will put the pig-tail in his pocket he likes pigtail, so ty it up. Dear Tom, shall be up about Monday there or thereabouts. Not so perticuler for the shirt, as the present can be washed, but dont forgit the pig-tail without fail, so am your loving brother,

Timothy Parsons.

P.S.—Dont forget the pig-tail.

————:o:————

Allusions to Tobacco in our Elizabethan literature are both numerous and interesting.

The early Dramatists delighted to honour the weed, yet curiously enough no mention of it occurs in the works of Shakespeare.

Poems and Ballads were soon sung in its praise, and naturally there were many whose distaste for smoking was also expressed in forcible terms.

The most noteworthy example of the latter was the ridiculous work written by the pedantic King James in 1603 entitled *A Counterblaste to Tobacco.*

Nearly all the great modern poets have been smokers, and have written in praise of its soothing effects, yet Swinburne, it is said, detests the habit and endorses the opinion expressed by King James :—

" *Surely smoke becomes a kitchen far better than a dining chamber, and yet it makes a kitchen oftentimes in the inward parts of men, soiling and infecting with an unctuous and oyly kind of soote as hath been found in some great tobacco takers that after death were opened.*

A custom loathsome to the eye, harmful to the braine,

*dangerous to the lungs, and in the black stinking fume
thereof, nearest resembling the horrible Stygian smoke of the
pit that is bottomless.''*

And later on he adds that, " *Tobacco is the lively image
and pattern of Hell.*"

The earliest printed verses on smoking with which I am
acquainted occur in a very rare little book, entitled : " *Dyet's
Dry Dinner,*" by H. Buttes, printed in 1599. The conversation it refers to appears to have taken place at a Theatre, in
which places of amusement smoking was largely indulged in
until comparatively modern times :—

A Satyricall Epigram upon the Wanton and Excessive Use of Tabacco.

It chaunc'd me gazing at the Theater,
To spie a Lock-Tabacco-Chevalier
Clowding the loathing ayr with foggie fume
Of Dock Tabacco friendly foe to rhume.
    I wisht the Roman Lawes severity
Who smoke selleth, with smoke be don to dye
Being well nigh smouldered with this smokie stir
I gan this wise bespeak my gallant Sir ;
Certes ! me thinketh, Sir, it ill beseems
Thus here to vapour out these reeking steams :
Like or Maroe's steeds, whose nostrils flamed
Or Plinies Nosemen (mouthless men) surnamed,
Whose breathing Nose supply'd mouth's absency.
    He me regreets with this prophane reply :—
"Nay, I resemble, Sir, Jehovah dread,
From out whose Nostrils a smoake issued ;
Or the mid ayrs congealed region,
Whose stomach with crude humours frozen on
Sucks up Tabacco like the upmost ayr.

Enkindled by Fire's neighbour Candle fayr.
And hence it spits out watery reums amaine
Or phleamy snow, and haile, and sheerer raine.
Anon it smoaks beneath, it flames anon.''

    Sooth then, quoth I, its safest we be gone,
    Lest there arise some Ignis Fatuus
From out this smoaking flame and choken us.

    On English foole : Wanton Italianly :
Go Frenchly : Dutchly drink : Breathe Indianly.

THE PRAISE OF TRINADADO. 1608.

COME, sirrah, Jacke hoe !
Fill some Tobacco ;
    Bring a wire
    And some fire
    Haste, Haste, away,
    Quicker, I say,
    Do not stay,
    Shun delay,
For I dranke none good today.
I swear that this tobacco
It's perfect Trinidado ;
By the very, very mass
Never was there better gere,
    Then is here.
    By the roode !
For the blood
'Tis very good.

Fill the pipe once more,
My brains dance *Trenchmore* ; *

---

* A popular dance of the period.

It is heady,
I am geddy,
My head and brains
Back and raines,
Joints and vaines,
From all paines
It doth well purge and make cleane.
Then those that doe condemn it,
Or such as not commend it,
Never were so wise to learne,
Good tobacco to discerne :
Let them go
Pluck a crow,
And not know as I do
The sweete of Trinidado.

From Weelkes' *Ayres, or Phantasticke Spirites*, 1608. At the period when this book was printed, the produce of the island of Trinidad was in great request by the race of smokers. Heylin, the old cosmographer, says that the island abounded in the best kind of tobacco, much celebrated formerly by the name of a " Pipe of Trinidado."

From the following passage in Ben Jonson's play, " The Alchemist," first acted in 1610, we gather some curious particulars respecting the business of a tobacconist of that period. It occurs in the first act, where Abel Drugger is introduced to Subtle :

" This is my friend Abel, an honest fellow ;
He lets me have good tobacco, and he does not
Sophisticate it with sack-lees or oil,
Nor washes it in muscadel and grains,
Nor buries it in gravel, underground,

Wrapt up in greasy leather, ...
But keeps it in fine lily pots that, open'd,
Smell like conserve of roses, or French beans,
He has his maple block, his silver tongs,
Winchester pipes, and fire of juniper :
A neat, spruce, honest fellow.   .   .

Some well-known lines in favour of smoking are often quoted, and *more frequently* misquoted, by people who have no idea of their antiquity.

"Much victuals serves for gluttony
    To fatten men like swine,
But he's a frugal man indeed
    That with a leaf can dine,
And needs no napkin for his hands
    His fingers ends to wipe,
But keeps his kitchen in a box,
    And roast meat in a pipe."

This passage occurs in the midst of a long speech in favour of tobacco, written by Samuel Rowlands in his *Knave of Clubbs* in 1611.

On Sunday the 26th August, 1621, a comedy, entitled "*Technogamia, or the Marriage of the Arts,*" written by Barton Holiday, M.A., of Christ's Church, Oxford, was performed by students of that college, before King James, at Woodstock. The King was much displeased with the play for the following reason :—

Phlegmaticus, one of the characters, entered exclaiming, "Fore Jove, most meteorological tobacco ! Pure Indian ! not a jot sophisticated ; a tobacco pipe is the chimney of

perpetual hospitality. Fore Jove, most metropolitan tobacco," and then broke out into the following song :—

TOBACCO's a Musician
And in a pipe delighteth ;
It descends in a close
Through the organs of the nose,
With a relish that inviteth.

This makes me sing so ho, so ho, boyes,
Ho boys sound I loudly.
Earth ne'er did breed
Such a jovial weed
Whereof to boast so proudly.

Tobacco is a Lawyer,
His pipes do love long cases,
When our brains it enters
Our feete do make indentures ;
While we seale with stamping paces.
Chorus.

Tobacco's a Physician,
Good both for sound and sickly,
'Tis a hot perfume,
That expels cold rheum,
And makes it flow downe quickly.
Chorus.

Tobacco is a Traveller,
Come from the Indies hither,
It passed sea and land
Ere it came to my hand,
And scaped the wind and weather.
Chorus.

Tobacco is a Critticke,
That still old paper turneth

B

Whose labour and care
Is as smoke in the aire
That ascends from a rag when it burneth.
                                    Chorus.

Tobacco's an ignis fatuus
A fat and fyrie vapour,
     That leads men about
     Till the fire be out,
Consuming like a taper.
                                    Chorus.

  Tobacco is a Whyffler,
     And cries " huff snuff " with furie,
          His pipes, his club, and linke,
          He's the wiser that does drinke
     Thus armed I fear not a furie.

This makes me sing so ho, so ho, boyes,
     Ho boys sound I loudly,
          Earth ne'er did breed
          Such a jovial weed
     Whereof to boast so proudly.

Prefixed to Rand's edition of Skelton's *Elinour Rumming*,
printed in 1624, are some verses curiously descriptive of the
then general habit of tobacco smoking :—

NOR did that time know
To puffe and to blow
In a peece of white clay,
As you doe at this day,
With fier and coale
And a leafe in a hole ;
As my ghost hath late seene,
As I walked between

Westminster Hall
And the Church of Saint Paul,
And so thorow the citie,
Where I saw and did pitty
My country men's cases,
With fiery-smoke faces, ,
Sucking and drinking
A filthie weede stinking,
Was ne'er knowne before
Till the devil and the More
In the Indies did meete,
And each other there greete
With a health they desire
Of stinke, smoke and fier.

These lines are supposed to be spoken by the ghost of
Skelton, who was Poet Laureate to Henry VIII.

THE TRYUMPH OF TOBACCO OVER SACK AND ALE.

From *Wits' Recreations,* 1640.

NAY, soft by your leaves,
Tobacco bereaves
You both of the garland, forbear it ;
You are two to one,
Yet tobacco alone
Is like both to win it and weare it.

Though many men crack,
Some of ale, some of sack,
And think they have reason to do it ;
Tobacco hath more
That will never give o'er
The honour they do unto it.

B 2

Tobacco engages
Both sexes, all ages,
   The poor as well as the wealthy ;
From the court to the cottage,
From childhood to dotage,
   Both those that are sick and the healthy.

It plainly appears
That in a few years
   Tobacco more custom hath gain'd
Than sack or than ale,
Though they double the tale
   Of the times wherein they have reign'd.

And worthily too,
For what they undo,
   Tobacco doth help to regain,
On fairer conditions
Than many physicians,
   Puts an end to much grief and pain.

It helpeth digestion,
Of that there's no question
   The gout and the toothache it eases ;
Be it early or late,
'Tis ne'er out of date,
   He may safely take it that pleases.

Tobacco prevents
Infection by scents,
   That hurt the brain and are heady,
An antidote is
Before you're amiss,
   As well as an after remedy.

The cold it doth heat,
Cools them that do sweat,
   And them that are fat maketh lean,
The hungry doth feed,
And if there be need,
   Spent spirits restoreth again.

Tobacco infused
May safely be used,
   For purging and killing of lice :
Not so much as the ashes,
But heals cuts and slashes,
   And that out of hand in a trice.

The Poets of old
Many Fables have told,
   Of the gods and their symposia,
But Tobacco alone,
Had they known it had gone,
   For their *Nectar* and *Ambrosia.*

It is not the smack
Of ale or of sack,
   That can with tobacco compare :
For taste and for smell,
It bears away the bell
   From them both, wherever they are.

For all their bravado
It is Trinidado,
   That both their noses will wipe
Of the praises they desire,
Unless they conspire
   To sing to the tune of his pipe.

A little book, published in the days of Queen Anne, entitled, "The True Trial of understanding, or Wit newly revived," contained the following riddle:

> "What tho' I have a nauseous breath,
>   Yet many a one will me commend;
> I am beloved after death,
>   And serviceable to my friend,"

to which is appended the answer, "This is tobacco after cut and dry'd, being dead becometh serviceable."

To three-fourths of a cross add a circle complete :	TO
Let two semicircles a perpendicular meet :	B
Next add a triangle that stands on two feet :	A
Then two semicircles, and a circle complete :	CCO

———:o:———

THE INDIAN WEED.

Many versions exist of the following very old song, and the history of it is somewhat contradictory and confusing. It has been ascribed to George Wither (1588—1667), and was originally published in 1631, in a volume entitled *The Soules Solace*, by Thomas Jenner. Another version was printed in 1672 in "Two Broadsides against Tobacco."

One version commenced with the following stanza:

> WHY should we so much despise
> So good and sweet an exercise
> As, early and late, to meditate?
>   Thus think, and drink tobacco.*

---

* The term "drinking" tobacco was commonly used in the early days of smoking.

The most usually accepted version runs as follows :—

THE Indian weed withered quite,
Green at noon, cut down at night,
    Shows thy decay,—
    All flesh is hay :
        Thus think, then drink tobacco.

The pipe that is so lily-white,
Shows thee to be a mortal wight,
    And even such,
    Gone with a touch :
        Thus think, then drink tobacco.

And when the smoke ascends on high,
Think thou behold'st the vanity
    Of worldly stuff,
    Gone with a puff :
        Thus think, then drink tobacco.

And when the pipe grows foul within,
Think on thy soul defiled with sin ;
    And then the fire
    It doth require :
        Thus think, then drink tobacco.

The ashes that are left behind,
May serve to put thee still in mind,
    That unto dust,
    Return thou must,
        Thus think, then drink tobacco.

The next is a more modern version :—

TOBACCO IS AN INDIAN WEED.

THIS Indian weed now withered quite
Though green at noon, cut down at night,

Shows thy decay ;
All flesh is hay ;
    Thus think, and smoke tobacco.

The pipe, so lily-like and weak,
Does thus thy mortal state bespeak ;
    Thou art e'en such,
    Gone with a touch :
    Thus think, and smoke tobacco.

And when the smoke ascends on high,
Then thou behold'st the vanity
    Of worldly stuff,
    Gone with a puff !
    Thus think, and smoke tobacco.

And when the pipe grows foul within,
Think on thy soul defiled with sin ;
    For then the fire
    It does require :
    Thus think, and smoke tobacco.

Thou seest the ashes cast away,
Then to thyself thou mayest say,
    That to the dust
    Return thou must :
    Thus think, and smoke tobacco.

Some additional, but very inferior stanzas,
were written by the Rev. Ralph Erskine, a
minister of the Scotch Church, and printed in

his *Gospel Sonnets,* about the end of the last century.   This continuation has been called

Smoking Spiritualized.

" Was this small plant for thee cut down?
So was the plant of great renown,
    Which mercy sends
    For nobler ends.
        Thus think and smoke tobacco.

" Doth juice medicinal proceed
From such a naughty foreign weed?
    Then what's the power
    Of Jesse's flower?
        Thus think and smoke tobacco.

" The promise, like the pipe, inlays
And, by the mouth of faith, conveys
    What virtue flows
    From Sharon's rose.
        Thus think and smoke tobacco.

" In vain th' unlighted pipe you blow,
Your pains in outward means are so,
    Till heavenly fire
    Your heart inspire.
        Thus think and smoke tobacco.

" The smoke, like burning incense, towers ;
So should a praying heart of yours
    With ardent cries
    Surmount the skies.
        Thus think and smoke tobacco.

A Catch on Tobacco.

(Sung by four men smoking their Pipes.)

Good, good indeed ;
The herb's good weed ;
Fill thy pipe, Will.
And I prithee, Sam, fill,
And yet sing still,
And yet sing still,
What say the learn'd ?
What say the learn'd ?
Vita fumus, vita fumus !

    'Tis what you and I,
    And he and I,
    You, and he, and I,
    And all of us *sumus.*

But then to the learned say we again,
If life's a smoke as they maintain ;
If life's a vapour without doubt,
    When a man does die,
    He should not cry,
That his glass is run but his pipe is out.
But whether we smoke or whether we sing,
Let us be loyal and remember the King,
Let him live, and let his foes vanish thus,
    thus, thus,
Like, like a pipe, like a pipe of Spanish,
    thus, thus, thus,
              A pipe of Spanish !

From "*Bacchus and Venus.*"   1737.

INVOCATION TO TOBACCO.

WEED of the strange power, weed of the earth,
Killer of dulness—parent of mirth;
Come in the sad hour, come in the gay,
Appear in the night, or in the day :
Still thou art welcome as June's blooming rose,
Joy of the palate, delight of the nose.

Weed of the green field, weed of the wild,
Foster'd in freedom, America's child ;
Come in Virginia, come in Havannah,
Friend of the universe, sweeter than manna :
Still thou art welcome, rich, fragrant and ripe.
Pride of the tube-case, Delight of the pipe.

Weed of the savage, weed of each pole,
Comforting,—soothing,—Philosophy's soul ;
Come in the snuff-box, Come in cigar,
In Strasburgh and King's, come from afar ;
Still thou art welcome, the purest, the best,
Joy of earth's millions, for ever carest.

From *Nicotiana,* by Henry James Meller. London
Effingham Wilson. 1832.

VIRGINIA TOBACCO.

Two maiden dames of sixty-two
Together long had dwelt :
Neither, alas ! of love so true,
The bitter pangs had felt.

But age comes on, they say, apace,
To warn us of our death,

And wrinkles mar the fairest face,
   At last it stops our breath.

One of these dames, tormented sore
   With that curst pang, tooth-ache,
Was at a loss for such a bore
   What remedy to take :

" I've heard," thought she, " this ill to cure,
   A pipe is good, they say,
Well then, tobacco I'll endure,
   And smoke the pain away."

The pipe was lit, the tooth soon well,
   And she retir'd to rest—
When thus the other ancient belle
   Her spinster mate addressed :—

" Let me request a favour, pray "—
   " I'll do it if I can "—
" Oh ! well then, love, smoke every day,
   You smell so like a man ! "

From *Gimcrackiana,* or Fugitive pieces on Manchester
Men and Manners. Manchester, 1833. (Attributed to
John Stanley Gregson.)

———

An Address to the Critics.

CRITICS avaunt—tobacco is my theme,
Tremble like hornets at the blasting steam ;
And you Court insects—flutter not too near
Its light, nor buzz within its scorching sphere.
Pollio, with flame like thine, my verse inspire,
So shall the Muse, with smoke, elicit fire ;
Coxcombs prefer the tickling sting of snuff,

Yet all their claim to wisdom is—a puff.
Lord Fopling smokes not—for his teeth afraid ;
Sir Tawdry smokes not—for he wears brocade.
Ladies, when pipes are brought, affect to swoon ;
They love no smoke, except the smoke of town.
But courtiers hate the puffing tribe—no matter,
Strange if they love the breath that cannot flatter.
Its foes but show their ignorance, can he
Who scorns the leaf of knowledge, love the tree ?

Citronia vows it has an odious stink,
She will not smoke, ye gods, but she will drink ;
And chaste Prudella—blame her if you can—
Says—pipes are used by that vile creature man.
Yet crowds remain, who still its worth proclaim,
For some for pleasure smoke, and some for fame—
Fame, of our actions, universal spring,
For which we drink, eat, sleep, smoke—everything.

Smoking and Smokers. By W. A. Delamotte. 1845.

A MANILLA SONNET.

LUSCIOUS leaf of fragrant savour,
Mild cheroot of choicest flavour,
Wafting incense to the sky,
Like the gales of Araby,
Let us press thee to our lips,
As the bee the honey sips ;
Culling as our well-earned meed,
Joys from thee—thou heavenly weed !
Ere thy burnished lip we kiss,
Let us thus enjoy the bliss,

Lit by the promethean spark,
Kindled from the congreve dark ;
In summer-house or country villa,
There's nothing like a good Manilla !

From *A Pipe of Tobacco*, by E. L. Blanchard. London.
H. Beal. (No date.)

L'HEUREUX FUMEUR.

CERTAIN fumeur courtisait une veuve,
Grâce à l'hymen, lorsqu'il fut dans ses lacs,
Pour te donner, lui dit-il, une preuve
De mon amour, je vais mettre en éclats
Si tu le veux, ma pipe toute neuve ;
—Non, non ; la pipe a pour toi trop d'appas ;
Je ne la crains que lorsque je suis grosse :
L'odeur m'en plait quand je ne la suis pas ;
Tu peux fumer. Notre époux, dans la Beauce
Comme héritier d'un oncle, avait des droits ;
Il part. Suivant des conseils maladroits,
Dans un procès chicaneau vous l'enfourne ;
Ce n'est qu'après absence de vingt mois,
Qu'à son logis un matin il retourne,
Pipe à la bouche. Oh ! qu'est ce que je vois ?
S'écria-t-il en rentrant ; quoi ! commode,
Console igi ! pendule, glace la ?
D'où viennent donc ces meubles à la mode ?
—D'un troc. Je vais te conter tout cela ;
Mais—mon mari—ta pipe m'incommode.

PONS DE VERDUN.

AN ENCOMIUM ON TOBACCO.

THRICE happy Isles that stole the world's delight
And thus produce so rich a Margarite !

It is the fountain whence all pleasure springs,
A potion for imperial and mighty kings.
He that is master of so rich a store
May laugh at Crœsus and esteem him poor ;
And with his smoky sceptre in his fist,
Securely flout the toiling Alchymist,
Who daily labours with a vain expense
In distillations of the Quintessence,
Not knowing that this golden Herb alone
Is the Philosopher's admired Stone.

It is a favour which the Gods doth please,
If they do feed on smoke, as Lucian says.
Therefore the cause that the bright sun doth rest
At the low point of the declining West—
When his oft wearied horses breathless pant—
Is to refresh himself with this sweet Plant,
Which wanton Thetis from the West doth bring,
To joy her love after his toilsome ring :
For 'tis a cordial for an inward smart,
As is Dictamnum* to the wounded hart.
It is the sponge that wipes out all our woe ;
'Tis like the thorn that doth on Pelion grow,
With which whoe'er his frost limbs anoints,
Shall feel no cold in fat, or flesh, or joints.
'Tis like the river, which whoe'er doth taste,
Forgets his present griefs and sorrows past,
Music, which makes grim thoughts retire,
And for a while cease their tormenting fire
Music, which forces beasts to stand at gaze,

---

* An herb with which the hart is said to cure its wounds.

And fills their senseless spirits with amaze—
Compared to this is like delicious strings,
Which sound but harshly while Apollo sings.

The train with this infumed, all quarrel ends
And fiercest foemen turn to faithful friends ;
The man that shall this smoky magic prove,
Will need no philtres to obtain his love.
Yet this sweet simple, by misordered use,
Death or some dangerous sickness may produce.
Should we not for our sustentation eat
Because a surfeit comes from too much meat ?
Should we not thirst with mod'rate drink repress,
Because a dropsy springs from such excess ?
So our fair Plant—that doth as needful stand
As heaven, or fire, or air, or sea, or land ;
As moon, or stars that rule the gloomy night,
Or sacred friendship or the sunny light—
Her treasured virtue in herself enrolls,
And leaves the evil to vainglorious souls.
And yet, who dies with this celestial breath,
Shall live immortal in a joyful death.
All goods, all pleasures, it in one can link—
'Tis physic, clothing, music, meat, and drink.

Gods would have revell'd at their feasts of Mirth
With this pure distillation of the earth ;
The marrow of the world, star of the West,
The Pearl whereby this lower Orb is blest ;
The joy of Mortals, Umpire of all strife,
Delight of Nature, Mithridate of Life ;
The daintiest dish of a delicious feast,
By taking which Man differs from a beast.

ANONYMOUS. TEMP., JAMES I.

From *The Smoker's Guide, Philosopher and Friend*, by a
veteran of Smokedom. London. Hardwicke and Bogue.

LORD BYRON ON TOBACCO.

BORNE from a short frail pipe which yet had blown
Its gentle odours over either zone,
And, puff'd where'er winds rise or waters roll,
Had wafted smoke from Portsmouth to the Pole,
Opposed its vapour as the lightning flash'd,
And reek'd, midst mountain-billows unabash'd,
To Æolus a constant sacrifice,
Thro' every change of all the varying skies.
And what was he who bore it ?   I may err,
But deem him sailor or philosopher.
SUBLIME TOBACCO ! which from East to West
Cheers the tar's labour, or the Turkman's rest ;
Which on the Moslem's ottoman divides
His hours, and rivals opium and his brides ;
Magnificent in Stamboul, but less grand,
Though not less loved, in Wapping or the Strand ;
Divine in hookahs, glorious in a pipe,
When tipp'd with amber, mellow, rich, and ripe ;
Like other charmers, wooing the caress,
More dazzlingly when daring in full dress ;
Yet thy true lovers more admire by far
Thy naked beauties—give me a cigar !

The Island.

With my pipe in one hand, and my jug in the other,
  I drink to my neighbours and friend ;
All my care in a whiff of tobacco I smother,
  For life, I know, shortly must end.

A Shield of Adamant.

For lack o'
Tobacco,
    I'd die;
For cigars
O ! my stars ,
    How I cry !
For a smoke is the shield
Before which troubles yield—
    Enabling us cares to defy !

E. H. S.

Epitaph

On a young lady who desired that Tobacco might be planted over her grave.

Let no cold marble o'er my body rise—
But only earth above, and sunny skies.
Thus would I lowly lie in peaceful rest,
Nursing the Herb Divine from out my breast.
Green let it grow above this clay of mine,
Deriving strength from strength that I resign.
So in the days to come, when I'm beyond
This fickle life, will come my lovers fond,
And gazing on the plant, their grief restrain
In whispering, " Lo ! dear Anna blooms again ! "

The Patriotic Smoker's Lament.

Tell me, shade of Walter Raleigh,
    Briton of the truest type,
When that too-devoted valet
    Quenched your first-recorded pipe,

Were you pondering the opinion,
  As you watched the airy coil,
That the virtue of Virginian
  Might be bred in British soil ?

You transplanted the potato :
  'Twas a more enduring gift
Than the wisdom of a Plato
  To our poverty and thrift.
That respected root has flourished
  Nobly for a nation's need ;
But our brightest dreams are nourished
  Ever on a foreign weed.

For the deepest meditation
  Of the philosophic scribe,
For the poet's inspiration,
  For the cynic's polished gibe,
We invoke narcotic nurses
  In their jargon from afar :
I indite these modest verses,
  On a polyglot cigar.

Leaf that lulls a Turkish Aga
  May a scholar's soul renew,
Fancy spring from Larranaga,
  History from honeydew.
When the teacher and the tyro
  Spirit-manna fondly seek,
'Tis the cigarette from Cairo
  Or a compound from the Greek.

But no British-born aroma
  Is fit incense to the Queen :
Nature gives her best diploma
  To the alien nicotine.

We are doomed to her ill-favour ;
  For the plant that's native grown
Has a patriotic flavour
  Too exclusively our own.

O my country, could your smoker
  Boast your " shag," or even "twist,"
Every man were mediocre
  Save the blest tobacconist !
He will point immortal morals,
  Make all common praises mute,
Who shall win our grateful laurels
  With a national cheeroot !

The St. James's Gazette.

ODE TO THE WEED.

WHEN happy quite and cosy grown,
  I feel for meditation ripe,
I need companionship, and so
  I take a pipe.

When from the irksome cares of life
  I pine to be removèd far,
They vex no longer if I light,
  A good cigar.

I realize what Eden was,
  (Or some faint semblance of it get)
When " she " is with me, and I light
  A cigarette.

Ah me ! how much the spirits bless
  Mankind.   I fail when I begin

To count thy many gifts to me
    Sweet "Nicotin."

I wonder oft as I enjoy
    Thy calm delights (and calm indeed),
How they can call thy resting place
    By name "a weed."

O, may the world in all its ills,
    Ne'er have this greatest to confess,
That is, that it should e'er become
    Tobaccoless.

R. W. ESSEX.

AMOURETTES OF A SMOKER.

I FLIRTED first with cigarettes
    One windy, wild March day ;
But found their fire, like fair coquettes,
    Too soon consume away.

And then I wooed the mild cheroot,
    As balmy as the south ;
Inserting, after much dispute,
    The big end in my mouth.

Awhile I dallied with cigars,
    Havanna's ripe brunettes ;
And wafted incense to the stars,
    In blue and spiral jets.

Shag, bird's-eye, twist, and negro-head
    This infant doth eschew ;
And cavendish he hath "cut" dead :
    But "*Chacun à son goût.*"

One Christmas on an ottoman
  I sat, and some turkey
A fair girl brought me in a can—
  Ister, a duck was she !

I bought a pipe, with amber tip,
  Of Moses Abrahams ;
Alas ! one day I let it slip—
  I'll love no more mere-shams !

Now, all my youthful amours o'er,
  I'm wed, and every day
With smoking holocausts adore
  An idol made of clay.

GEORGE HILL.

A Farewell to Tobacco.

May the Babylonish curse
Straight confound my stammering verse,
If I can a passage see
In this word-perplexity,
Or a fit expression find,
Or a language to my mind
(Still the phrase is wide or scant),
To take leave of thee, Great Plant !
Or in any terms relate
Half my love or half my hate :
For I hate, yet love thee, so,
That, whichever thing I show,
The plain truth will seem to be
A constrain'd hyperbole,
And the passion to proceed
More from a mistress than a weed.
Sooty retainer to the vine,

Bacchus' black servant, negro fine ;
Sorcerer, that makèst us dote upon
Thy begrimed complexion,
And for thy pernicious sake,
More and greater oaths to break
Than reclaimed lovers take
'Gainst women : thou thy siege dost lay
Much too in the female way,
While thou suck'st the labouring breath
Faster than kisses or than death.

Thou in such a cloud dost bind us,
　That our worst foes cannot find us,
　And ill fortune, that would thwart us,
　Shoots at rovers, shooting at us ;
　While each man, through thy heightening steam,
　Does like a smoking Etna seem,
　And all about us does express
　(Fancy and wit in richest dress)
　A Sicilian fruitfulness.

Thou through such a mist dost show us,
　That our best friends do not know us,
　And, for those allowèd features,
　Due to reasonable creatures,
　Liken'st us to fell Chimeras—
　Monsters that, who see us, fear us ;
　Worse than Cerberus or Geryon,
　Or, who first loved a cloud, Ixion.

Bacchus we know, and we allow
　His tipsy rites.　But what art thou,
　That but by reflex canst show
　What his deity can do,
　As the false Egyptian spell
　Aped the true Hebrew miracle

Some few vapours thou may'st raise,
The weak brain may serve to amaze,
But to the reins and nobler heart
Canst nor life nor heat impart.

Brother of Bacchus, later born,
The old world was sure forlorn
Wanting thee, that aidest more
The god's victories than before
All his panthers, and the brawls
Of his piping Bacchanals.
These, as stale, we disallow,
Or judge of *thee* meant : only thou
His true Indian conquest art ;
And, for ivy round his dart
The reformèd god now weaves
A finer thyrsus of thy leaves.

Scent to match thy rich perfume
Chemic art did ne'er presume
Through her quaint alembic strain,
None so sovereign to the brain.
Nature, that did in thee excel,
Framed again no second smell.
Roses, violets, but toys,
For the smaller sort of boys,
Or for greener damsels meant ;
Thou art the only manly scent.

Stinking'st of the stinking kind,
Filth of the mouth and fog of the mind,
Africa, that brags her foison,
Breeds no such prodigious poison,
Henbane, nightshade, both together,
Hemlock, aconite—
                    Nay, rather,

Plant divine, of rarest virtue ;
Blisters on the tongue would hurt you.
'Twas but in a sort I blamed thee,
None e'er prosper'd who defamed thee :
Irony all, and feign'd abuse,
Such as perplex'd lovers use
At a need, when, in despair
To paint forth their fairest fair,
Or in part but to express
That exceeding comeliness
Which their fancies doth so strike,
They borrow language of dislike ;
And, instead of Dearest Miss,
Jewel, Honey, Sweetheart, Bliss,
And those forms of old admiring,
'Call her Cockatrice and Siren,
Basilisk, and all that's evil,
Witch, Hyena, Mermaid, Devil,
Ethiop, Wench, and Blackamoor,
Monkey, Ape, and twenty more :
Friendly Traitress, Loving Foe,—
Not that she is truly so,
But no other way they know
A contentment to express,
Borders so upon excess,
That they do not rightly wot
Whether it be pain or not.

Or as men, constrain'd to part,
With what's nearest to their heart,
While their sorrow's at the height,
Lose discrimination quite,
And their hasty wrath let fall,
To appease their frantic gall,
On the darling thing whatever,

Whence they feel it death to sever,
Though it be, as they. perforce,
Guiltless of the sad divorce.

For I must (nor let it grieve thee,
Friendliest of plants, that I must) leave thee.
For thy sake, Tobacco, I,
Would do anything but die,
And but seek to extend my days
Long enough to sing thy praise.
But, as she, who once hath been
A king's consort, is a queen
Ever after, nor will bate
Any tittle of her state
Though a widow, or divorced,
So I, from thy converse forced,
The old name and style retain,
A right Katherine of Spain :
And a seat, too, 'mongst the joys
Of the blest Tobacco Boys ;
Where, though I, by sour physician,
Am debarr'd the full fruition
Of thy favours, I may catch
Some collateral sweets, and snatch
Sidelong odours, that give life
Like glances from a neighbour's wife ;
And still live in the by-places
And the suburbs of thy graces ;
And in thy borders take delight
An unconquer'd Canaanite.

CHARLES LAMB.

TO

the very dear and well-beloved

𝔉𝔯𝔦𝔢𝔫𝔡

of my prosperous and evil days—

TO THE FRIEND

who, though, in the early stages of our acquaintanceship,
did ofttimes disagree with me, has since become
to be my very warmest comrade—

TO THE FRIEND

who, however often I may put him out, never (now)
upsets me in revenge—

TO THE FRIEND

who, treated with marked coldness by all the female
members of my household, and regarded with
suspicion by my very dog, nevertheless, seems day by day
to be more drawn by me, and, in return, to
more and more impregnate me with the
odour of his friendship—

TO THE FRIEND

who never tells me of my faults, never wants to borrow
money, and never talks about himself—
To the companion of my idle hours,
the soother of my sorrows,
the confidant of my joys and hopes—
My oldest and strongest

PIPE,

THIS LITTLE VOLUME

is

gratefully and affectionately
dedicated.

(Dedication to "The Idle Thoughts of an Idle Fellow,
a Book for an Idle Holiday." By Jerome K. Jerome,
London, Field & Tuer, 1887.)

POEMS ON THE PIPE.

HAIL! social pipe—thou foe to care,
Companion of my elbow chair;
As forth thy curling fumes arise,
They seem an evening sacrifice—
An offering to my Maker's praise,
For all His benefits and grace.

DR. GARTH.

SONNET TO A PIPE. (1690.)

"Doux charme de ma solitude,
Brulante pipe, ardent fourneau!
Qui purges d'humeur mon cerveau,
Èt mon esprit d'ínquietude.
Tabac! dont mon ame est ravie,

Lorsque je te vois te perdre en l'air,
Aussi promptement q'un éclair,
Je vois l'image de ma vie ;
Tu remets dans mon souvenir,
Ce qu'un jour je dois devenir,
N'étant qu'une cendre animée ;
Et tout d'un coup je m'aperçoi,
Que courant aprés ta fumée,
Je passe de même que toi.''

Attributed to *Esprit de Raymond, Comte de Modène.*

Translation of the above.

'' SWEET smoking pipe, bright glowing stove,
Companion still of my retreat,
Thou dost my gloomy thoughts remove,
And purge my brain with gentle heat.

'' Tobacco, charmer of my mind,
When, like the meteor's transient gleam
Thy substance gone to air I find,
I think, alas ! my life the same.

'' What else but lighted dust am I ?
Thou show'st me what my fate will be ;
And when thy sinking ashes die,
I learn that I must end like thee.''

TO A PIPE OF TOBACCO.

COME, lovely tube by friendship blest,
   Belov'd and honour'd by the wise,
Come, fill'd with honest *Weekly's best,*
   And kindled from the lofty skies.

While round me clouds of incense roll,
  With guiltless joys you charm the sense,
And nobler pleasures to the soul,
  In hints of moral truth, dispense.

Soon as you feel th' enlivening ray,
  To dust you hasten to return ;
And teach me that my earliest day,
  Began to give me to the urn.

But tno' thy grosser substance sink
  To dust, thy purer part aspires ;
This when I see, I joy to think
  That earth but half of me requires.

Like thee myself am born to die,
  Made half to rise and half to fall.
O ! could I while my moments fly,
  The bliss you give me, give to all.

From *The Gentleman's Magazine.*   July, 1746.

CHOOSING A WIFE BY A PIPE OF TOBACCO.

  TUBE, I love thee as my life ;
  By thee I mean to chuse a wife,
  Tube, thy *colour* let me find,
  In her *skin* and in her *mind*
  Let her have a *shape* as fine ;
  Let her breath be sweet as thine :
  Let her, when her lips I kiss,
  Burn like thee, to give me bliss :
  Let her in some *smoke* or other,
  All my failings kindly smother.
  Often when my thoughts are *low,*

Send them where they *ought to go.*
When to study I incline
Let her aid be such as thine :
Such as thine her charming pow'r,
In the vacant social hour
Let her live to give delight,
Ever *warm* and ever *bright :*
Let her deeds, whene'er she dies,
Mount as *incense to the skies.*

From *The Gentleman's Magazine.* 1757.

TRANSLATION OF A GERMAN SONG.

WHEN my pipe burns bright and clear,
  The gods I need not envy here ;
And as the smoke fades in the wind,
  Our fleeting life it brings to mind.

Noble weed ! that comforts life,
  And art with calmest pleasures rife ;
Heaven grant thee sunshine and warm rain,
  And to thy planter health and gain.

Through thee, friend of my solitude,
  With hope and patience I'm endued,
Deep sinks thy power within my heart,
  And cares and sorrows all depart.

Then let non-smokers rail for ever ;
  Shall their hard words true friends dissever ?
Pleasure's too rare to cast away
  My pipe, for what the railers say !

When love grows cool, thy fire still warms me.
　When friends are fled, thy presence charms me ;
If thou art full, though purse be bare,
　I smoke, and cast away all care !

THE PIPE OF TOBACCO.

WHY should life in sorrow be spent,
　When pleasure points to the road
Wherein each traveller with content
　May throw off the ponderous load?

And instead, in ample measure,
　Gather fruits too long left ripe ;
What's this world without its pleasure?
　What is pleasure but a pipe?

See the sailor's jovial state,
　Mark the soldier's noble soul ;
What doth heroes renovate ?
　What refines the splendid bowl ?

Is it not tobacco dear,
　That from the brow fell grief can wipe ?
Yes ! like them with jolly cheer,
　I find pleasure in a pipe.

Some are fond of care and grief,
　Some take pleasure in sad strife,
Some pursue a false belief—
　Few there are that enjoy life.

Some delight in envy ever,
  Others avaricious gripe ;
Would you know our greatest pleasure?
  'Tis a glowing social pipe.
    (Printed by W. J. Shelmerdine, about 1794.)
From Logan's *Pedlar's Pack of Ballads*.

LA PIPE DE TABAC.

CONTRE les chagrins de la vie,
  On crie, " Et ab hoc et ab hac ; "
Moi, je me crois digne d'envie,
  Quand j'ai ma pipe et mon tabac.
Aujourd'hui, changeant de folie,
  Et de boussole et d'almanach,
Je préfère fille jolie,
  Même à la pipe de tabac.

Le soldat bâille sous la tente,
  Le matelot sur le tillac ;
Bientot ils ont l'âme contente,
  Avec la pipe de tabac.
Si pourtant survient une belle
  À l'instant le cœur fait tictac,
Et l'amant oublie auprès d'elle
  Jusqu'à la pipe de tabac.

Je tiens cette maxime utile
  De ce fameux monsieur de Crac :
En campagne, comme à la ville,
  Fêtons l'amour et le tabac.
Quand ce grand homme allait en guerre,
  Il portait dans son petit sac,
Le doux portrait de sa bergère,
  Avec la pipe de tabac.
           PIGAULT LEBRUN.   (1755—1835.

CONTENT AND A PIPE.

CONTENTED I sit with my pint and my pipe,
  Puffing sorrow and care far away,
And surely the brow of grief nothing can wipe
  Like smoking and moist'ning our clay ;
For, though liquor can banish man's reason afar,
  'Tis only a fool or a sot,
Who with reason or sense would be ever at war,
  And don't know when enough he has got.
For, though at my simile many may joke,
Man is but a pipe—and his life but smoke.

Yes, a man and a pipe are much nearer akin
  Than has as yet been understood,
For, until with breath they are both fill'd within,
  Pray tell me for what are they good ?
They, one and the other, composed are of clay,
  And, if rightly I tell nature's plan,
Take but the breath from them both quite away,
  The pipe dies and so does the man :
For, though at my simile many may joke,
Man is but a pipe—and his life but smoke.

Thus I'm told by my pipe that to die is man's lot,
  And, sooner or later, die he must ;
For when to the end of life's journey he's got,
  Like a pipe that's smoked out—he is dust :
So you, who would wish in your hearts to be gay,
  Encourage not strife, care, or sorrow,
Make much of your pipe of tobacco to-day,
  For you may be smoked out to-morrow :
For, though at my simile many may joke,
  Man is but a pipe--and his life but smoke.

To the Tobacco Pipe.

DEAR piece of fascinating clay !
'Tis thine to smooth life's rugged way,
To give a happiness unknown,
To those—who let a pipe alone ;
Thy tube can best the vapours chase,
By raising—others in their place ;
Can give the face staid wisdom's air,
And teach the lips—to ope with care ;
'Tis hence thou art the truest friend,
(Where least is said there's least to mend,)
And he who ventures many a joke
Had better oft be still and smoke.

Whatever giddy foplings think,
Thou giv'st the highest zest to drink
When fragrant clouds thy fumes exhale,
And hover round the nut-brown ale,
Who thinks of claret or champagne ?
E'en burgundy were pour'd in vain.

'Tis not in city smoke alone
'Midst fogs and glooms thy charms are known.
With thee, at morn, the rustic swain
Tracks o'er the snow-besprinkled plain,
To seek some neighb'ring copse's side,
And rob the woodlands of their pride ;
With thee, companion of his toil,
His active spirits ne'er recoil ;
Though hard his daily task assign'd,
He bears it with an equal mind.

The fisher, 'board some little bark,
When all around is drear and dark

With shortened pipe beguiles the hour,
Though bleak the wind, and cold the show'r ;
Nor thinks the morn's approach too slow,
Regardless of what tempests blow.
Midst hills of sand, midst ditches, dykes,
Midst cannons, muskets, halberts, pikes ;
With thee, as still, Mynheer can stay,
As Neddy 'twixt too wisps of hay ;
Heedless of Britain and of France,
Smokes on—and looks to the main chance.

And sure the solace thou canst give,
Must make thy fame unrivalled live,
So long as men can temper clay,
(For as thou art, e'en so are they,)
The sun mature the Indian weed,
And rolling years fresh sorrows breed !

From *The Meteors.* London : A. & J. Black. 1800.

SAYS THE PIPE TO THE SNUFF-BOX.

SAYS the Pipe to the Snuff-box, "I can't understand
  What the ladies and gentlemen see in your face,
That you are in fashion all over the land,
  And I am so much fallen into disgrace.

"Do but see what a pretty contemplative air
  I give to the company—pray do but note 'em,—
You would think that the wise men of Greece were all there
  Or, at least, would suppose them the wise men of Gotham.

"My breath is as sweet as the breath of blown roses,
  While you are a nuisance where'er you appear ;

There is nothing but snivelling and blowing of noses,
  Such a noise as turns any man's stomach to hear."

Then lifting his lid in a delicate way,
  And opening his mouth with a smile quite engaging,
The Box in reply was heard plainly to say,
  "What a silly dispute is this we are waging!

"If you have a little of merit to claim,
  You may thank the sweet-smelling Virginian weed;
And I, if I seem to deserve any blame,
  The before-mention'd drug in apology plead.

"Thus neither the praise nor the blame is our own
  No room for a sneer, much less a cachinnus;
We are vehicles not of tobacco alone,
  But of anything else they may choose to put in us."

WILLIAM COWPER. 1782.

LA FEMME ET LA PIPE.

PLAINS-moi, Philippe, mon ami;
Le sort me traite en ennemi.
Un instant mon âme charmée
Sut se caresser de fumée;
Un instant m'enivra l'amour:
Hélas! tout a fui sans rétour.
Suis-je donc né pour le malheur, Philippe?
J'ai perdu ma femme et j'ai cassé ma pipe.
Ah! combien je regrette ma pipe!

Ma femme était blanche de peau,
Ma pipe était comme un corbeau;
Elle était simple et pas bégueule;

Je m'en servais en brûle-gueule :
Avec elles deux je chauffais
Mon lit, mes doigts et mon palais !
Suis-je donc né pour le malheur, etc.

La femme veut des petits soins,
Et la pipe n'en veut pas moins :
Je bourrais ma chère compagne
D'amour, de gâteaux, de champagne ;
Je bourrais ma pipe souvent
Du fameux tabac du Levant.
Suis-je donc né, etc.

Dans le quartier était cité
Notre charmante trinité.
Quand dans la rue ou sur les places
Tous trois nous étalions nos grâces,
L'une sur mon bras se pressait,
L'autre à ma bouche se plaçait.
Suis-je donc né, etc.

Quand, par un caprice à blâmer,
Ma femme me faisait fumer,
Moi, j'avais alors un principe ;
Je prenais ma blague et ma pipe,
Et, las de fumer au moral,
Je savourais mon caporal.
Suis-je donc né, etc.

Ma femme avait bien des appas,
Et ma pipe n'en manquait pas.
Que sa jupe était bien portée !
Dieu ! qu'elle était bien culottée !
J'embrassais l'une en musulman,
Je fumais l'autre en Allemand.
Suis-je donc né, etc.

Conclusion Consolante.

—Mon cher Fumard, pour ton chagrin
Il est un baume ; c'est du vin !
La femme pour qui tu sanglotes,
Souvent te tirait des carottes,
Et grâce à la pipe, au tabac,
Se desséchait ton estomac.
—Tu crois ! allons, verse-moi donc, Philippe,
Verse-moi l'oubli de ma femme et ma pipe !
Ah ! pourtant je regrette ma pipe !

A POT AND A PIPE OF TOBACCO.

SOME praise taking snuff,
And 'tis pleasant enough,
To those who have got the right knack, oh !
But give me, my boys,
Those exquisite joys,
A pot and a pipe of tobacco.

When fume follows fume
To the top of the room,
In circles pursuing their track, O !
How sweet to inhale
The health-giving gale,
Of a pipe of Virginia tobacco.

Let soldiers, so bold,
For fame, or for gold,
Their enemies cut, slash, and hack, O !
We have fire and smoke
Though all but in joke,
In a peaceable pipe of tobacco.

Should a mistress unkind,
Be inconstant in mind,
And on your affections look black, O !
Let her werritt and tiff
'Twill blow off in a whiff,
If you take but a pipe of tobacco.

The miserly elf
Who, in hoarding his pelf,
Keeps body and soul on the rack, O !
Would he bless and be blest
He might open his chest,
By taking a pipe of tobacco.

Life's short, 'tis agreed
So we'll try from the weed,
Of man a brief emblem to tack, O !
When his spirit ascends,
Die he must—and he ends
In dust like a pipe of tobacco !

To an Old Pipe.

ONCE your smoothly-polished face
Nestled lightly in a case ;
'Twas a jolly, cosy place,
    I surmise ;
And a zealous subject blew
On your cheeks, until they grew
To the fascinating hue
    Of her eyes.

Near a rusty-hilted sword,
Now upon my mantle-board,
Where my curios are stored,
    You recline.
You were pleasant company when
By the scribbling of her pen
I was sent the ways of men
    To repine.

Tell me truly (you were there
When she ceased that debonair
Correspondence and affair)—
    I suppose
That she laughed and smiled all day ;
Or did gentle teardrops stray
Down her charming, *retrousée*,
    Little Rose ?

Where the sunbeams, coyly chill,
Fall upon the mantel-sill
You perpetually will
    Silence woo ;
And I fear that she herself,
By the little chubby elf,
Will be laid upon the shelf,
    Just as you.

            DE WITT STERRY.

THE CUTTY.

WHEN nobs come oot to walk aboot,
    And show their shapes to leddies ;
They're ne'er without their grand cheroot,
    Fer that they think well bred is.

And when they meet—no in the street,
  But aiblins ower a meal like—
Then oot they draw a meerschaum braw,
  An' that looks real genteel like.

Weel! there's nae ban on ony man,
  Let him be braw or sootie ;
I'll no debar their grand cigar,
  But I'll haud to my cutty.

   *   *   *   *

The winter's blast, aft gey an fast,
  Blaws your genteel cigar oot ;
My cutty's fire, with tap o' wire,
  Burns no a grain the waur o't.

   *   *   *   *

So now I'll ripe my cutty pipe,
  And bauldly face rude Boreas ;
And, as I fill, ower ilka ill,
  I'll still haud on victorious.

These extracts are taken from *A Pedlar's Pack of Ballads and Songs.* Edinburgh, W. Paterson. 1869.

MY CLAY PIPE.

" THOU cheering friend of many a weary hour,
  I'll sing thy virtues in my humble lay ;
Oft have I felt thy gentle, soothing power ;
  I do not scorn thee, though thou art but *clay.*

Far dearer thou to me than choicest work
   From the skill'd products of Italia's land,
Or rich chibouque of the enamour'd Turk,
   With endless tubes, and amber mouthpiece grand.

Companion thou hast been for many a year ;
   'Tis I have colour'd thy once fair face black ;
I could not leave thee now without a tear,
   Thou, the last keepsake of my old friend Jack.

He prized thee for thy shape—and then to hear
   How oft upon thy merits he hath spoken !
Long may I smoke thee with my evening beer,
   My own loved pipe !—Confound it ! it is broken ! "

On the Pleasure of a Pipe.

   CHARM of the solitude I love ;
      My pleasing, my glowing stove !
      My head of rheum is purged by thee ;
      My heart of vain anxiety.
      Tobacco ! favourite of my soul !
      When round my head thy vapours roll ;
      When lost in air they vanish too,
      An emblem of my life I view.
      I view, and, hence instructed, learn
      To what myself shall shortly turn :
      Myself, a kindled coal to-day,
      That wastes in smoke, and flees away.
      Swiftly as these—confusing thought—
      Alas ! I vanish into naught.

From *Cope's Tobacco Plant.*   December, 1871.

LA PIPE.

JE suis la pipe d un auteur ;
On voit, à contempler ma mine
D'Abyssinienne ou de Cafrine,
Que mon maitre est un grand fumeur.

Quand il est comblé de douleur,
Je fume comme la chaumine
Où se prépare la cuisine
Pour le retour du laboureur.

J'enlace et je berce son âme
Dans le réseau mobile et bleu
Qui monte de ma bouche en feu,

Et je roule un puissant dictame
Qui charme son cœur et guérit
De ses fatiques son esprit.

CHARLES BAUDELAIRE.

Translation of the above.

A POET'S pipe am I ;
And my Abyssinian tint
Is an unmistakable hint
That he lays me not often by,

When his soul is with grief o'erworn,
I smoke like the cottage where
They are cooking the evening fare
For the labourer's return.

I enfold and cradle his soul
In the vapour moving and blue
That mounts from my fiery mouth ;

And there is power in my bowl
To charm his spirit and soothe,
And heal his weariness too.

RICHARD HERNE SHEPHERD.

MY DARLING PIPE.

PIPE, my darling,
Fate is snarling—
      Let her snarl.

Thou art my love
Thee do I love
      Best of all.

In thy kisses,
Truest blisses
      Ever dwell.

Faithful ever,
Pouting never—
      Ah ! 'tis well,

Pipe, my darling,
Fate is snarling—
      Let her snarl

————:o:————

MY AFTER-DINNER CLOUD.

SOME sombre evening, when I sit
   And feed in solitude at home,
Perchance an ultra-bilious fit
   Paints all the world an orange chrome.

When Fear, and Care, and grim Despair,
  Flock round me in a ghostly crowd,
One charm dispels them all in air ;—
  I blow my after-dinner cloud.

'Tis melancholy to devour
  The gentle chop in loneliness.
I look on six—my prandial hour—
  With dread not easy to express.
And yet, for every penance done,
  Due compensation seems allow'd,
My penance o'er, its price is won ;—
  I blow my after-dinner cloud.

My clay is *not* a Henry Clay—
  I like it better, on the whole ;
And when I fill it, I can say
  I drown my sorrows in the bowl.
For most I love my lowly pipe
  When weary, sad, and leaden-brow'd :
At such a time behold me ripe
  To blow my after-dinner cloud.

As gracefully the smoke ascends
  In columns from the weed beneath,
My friendly wizard, Fancy lends
  A vivid shape to every wreath.
Strange memories of life or death,
  Up from the cradle to the shroud,
Come forth as, with enchanter's breath,
  I blow my after-dinner cloud.

What wonder if it stills my care
  To quit the present for the past ;

And summon back the things that were,
  Which only thus in vapour last ?
What wonder if I envy not
  The rich, the giddy, and the proud,
Contented in this quiet spot
  To blow my after-dinner cloud ?

From *Gillott and Goosequill.*   By Henry S. Leigh.
London, British Publishing Company.   1871.

My Three Loves.

When Life was all a summer day,
  And I was under twenty,
Three loves were scattered in my way—
  And three at once are plenty.
Three hearts, if offered with a grace,
  One thinks not of refusing.
The task in this especial case
  Was only that of choosing.
      I knew not which to make my pet—
      My pipe, cigar, or cigarette.

To cheer my night or glad my day
  My pipe was ever willing ;
The meerschaum or the lowly clay
  Alike repaid the filling.
Grown men delight in blowing clouds,
  As boys in blowing bubbles,
Our cares to puff away in crowds,
  And banish all our troubles.
      My pipe I nearly made my pet,
      Above cigar or cigarette.

A tiny paper, tightly rolled
  About some Latakia,

Contains within its magic fold
   A mighty *panacea*.
Some thought of sorrow or of strife
   At ev'ry whiff will vanish ;
And all the scenery of life
   Turn picturesquely Spanish.
      But still I could not quite forget
      Cigar and pipe for cigarette.

To yield an after-dinner puff
   O'er *demi-tasse* and brandy,
No cigarettes are strong enough
   No pipes are ever handy.
However fine may be the feed,
   It only moves my laughter
Unless a dry delicious weed
   Appears a little after.
      A prime cigar I firmly set
      Above a pipe or cigarette.

But, after all, I try in vain
   To fetter my opinion ;
Since each upon my giddy brain
   Has boasted a dominion.
Comparisons I'll not provoke,
   Lest *all* should be offended.
Let this discussion end in smoke,
   As many more have ended.
      And each I'll make a special pet ;
      My pipe, cigar, and cigarette.

               HENRY S. LEIGH.

The London Magazine.   November, 1875.

———— :o: ————

                    F.

ODE TO MY PIPE.

My pipe to me, thro' gloom and glee,
  Has been my faithful friend ;
I sit and *smoke*—not sit and soak,
  For that I can't commend.

Bird's eye, returns, or shag that burns
  Most freely and most bright ;
This Indian weed, it is, indeed,
  My solace and delight.

Some people say it steals away
  The brain, till all is bare,
But they are foes, or *chiefly* those
  Who've got no brains to spare.

Great Doctor Parr, bright learning's star,
  A scholar rare and ripe,
Would sit and puff, through smooth and rough,
  Enraptured with his pipe.

My pipe I'll fill, and smoke I will,
  Though all the world condemn ;
And if I die burnt black and dry,
  Pray, what is that to them ?

The Echo.   February 16, 1889.

WHO SCORNS THE PIPE.

Who scorns the pipe ?   Show me the man,
  I do not mention " glasses,"
He's writhing under social ban
  The jink his soul compasses—
                Old friend Tobacco !

Ye carping souls, who, envious, doom
  The weed to dire perdition,
Just take a whiff—dispel the gloom
  That clouds your mental vision—
          Of rare Tobacco !

On a Broken Pipe.

Neglected now it lies a cold clay form,
So late with living inspirations warm :
Type of all other creatures formed of clay—
What more than it for epitaph have they ?

From *A Voice from the Nile*, by James Thomson. 1884.

———:o:———

Motto for a Tobacco Jar.

Come ! don't refuse sweet Nicotina's aid,
  But woo the goddess through a yard of clay ;
And soon you'll own she is the fairest maid
  To stifle pain and drive old Care away.
Nor deem it waste, what though to ash she burns,
  If for your outlay you get good Returns !

Some time since, in *Cope's Tobacco Plant*, there was a competition for the best inscription for a Tobacco Jar. The first and second prizes were awarded to the following, and many others were printed :—

First.

Inscription for a Tobacco Jar.

Three hundred year ago or soe,
  Ane worthye knight and gentleman

F. 2

Did bring mee here, to charm and cheer
  Ye physical and mental man.
God rest his soul, who filled ye bowl,
  And may our blessings find him ;
That hee not miss some share of bliss,
  Who left soe much behind him !

      Ye Smoke Jack (Bernard Barker).

Second.

Keep me at hand, and as my fumes arise
  You'll find *a jar* the gates of Paradise.

———:o:———

"*The Shrubs of Parnassus.* Consisting of a Variety of Poetical Essays, Moral and Comic. By *J. Copywell,* f Lincoln's Inn, Esq. ; London. Printed for the author ; and sold by J. Newbery, at the *Bible and Sun*, in St. Paul's Church-yard, 1760." Such is the title of a small volume of miscellaneous poems, in my copy of which it is stated that William Woty was the real author of most of the pieces, a few having been contributed by John Coppinger. It contains an address in blank verse to

The Tobacco-Stopper.

I, Who of late the useful cork-screw sung,
Or strove to sing, and in poetic verse
Immortaliz'd the Tankard, now prepare
Alike to magnify that engine small,
Tobacco-stopper hight, associate fit
For pipe-enamour'd Toper. Bless'd with thee
How careless does he sit, lolling at ease
Across the summit of contiguous chair.
Through the dark alley of the curving tube

The flavour of the burning weed he draws,
And at each puff he teaches ev'ry cloud
In what due poize to ride athwart the air,
Or curl its spiral head.   *   *   *   *

  *   *   *   *   *   *   *

This volume also contains " A Pinch of Snuff," which is
quoted further on.

———

HEIGHO 'BACCY.

(Ode on an Empty Pipe.   By a Hard-up Smoker.)

PLEASANT pipe, companionable clay !
  Empty—like thy luckless master's pocket,
Fireless as Care's candle burned away,
  Long ere daybreak, to the very socket !
When a cove is penniless and dry,
  Having whiffed the last of his small whack, he
Can do nought but pouch his pipe, and cry,
          Heigho 'Baccy,

Heigho 'Baccy ! I can understand
  How the " lag " in lonely cells longs for thee ;
How the storm-tost sailor, far from land,
  Yearns in night's long watch to "blow" or "chor"
      thee.
Comfortable weed ! Out on the churls,
  Scientific prigs, and sawbones quacky,
Who finds mischief in thy fragrant whirls,
          Heigho 'Baccy !

When the tinless toiler draws his belt
  With trembling hand a trifle tighter
To compress that vacuum each has felt
  Who with poverty has been a fighter,

If his lips may but caress his clay,
  Though cash will not run to glass or snack, he,
With recovered pluck can peg away.
          Heigho 'Baccy!

When cold Care confronts one in life's road,
  When bereavement chills the lonely ingle,
When sharp disappointment wields its goad,
  When a chap is seedy, stumped, sad, single,
Then, however sage ones chide or croak,
  Spite of doctor harsh, fanatic, cracky,
There *is* comfort in a quiet smoke!
          Heigho 'Baccy!

Punch, December 1, 1888.

PIPES AND PREJUDICE.

["It will be admitted by every unprejudiced man that
the use of tobacco is opposed to the instincts of our nature,
to the laws of our constitution, and to the designs of a
beneficent Creator."—Dr. RICHARD MARTIN.]

ADMIT it? No! We never will
  By such admissions damn our soul!
  Tobacco is, upon the whole,
Life's greatest good, or lightest ill.

The smiling optimist finds joys
  More joyful, seen through smoky haze;
  The smoking pessimist surveys
More patiently life's worthless toys.

The poet, painter, patriot, peer
  To smoke their inspiration owe:

Its magic qualities they know—
More fine than tea, more strong than beer !

The weary husband, tired of strife,
 " Lights up," and bears to "let things slide."
 How smoothly household wheels would glide
If guided by a smoking wife !

Tobacco, democratic weed,
 The prejudice that libels thee,
 Thou friend of rich and poor, must be
Colossal prejudice indeed !

Each to his taste, though ! If the true
 Pure joys of smoking cheer my way,
 Then Dr. Richard Martin may
Abuse my pipe till all is blue.

And as for prejudice !—We'll make
 This one "admission." In our eyes,
 In point of foolish prejudice
Your anti-smoker takes the cake !

E. B.

The Weekly Dispatch. February 24, 1889.

On a Tobacco Box.

WHOEVER in a mean abode presumes
To lodge that sacred herb, whose curling fumes
(More grateful than *Sabæan* odours far)
Play round the nose, and wanton in the air ;
May Æsculapius let him always want
The virtues of the health-restoring Plant ;
Or let th' unworthy sinner be confin d

To abject weeds of some *Plebeian* kind.
Bacchus his herb should have for its abode
The workmanship of the *Ætnean* God,
Well polisht steel, that, like the mimick glass,
Reflects the image of the smoaker's face,
And lets him see how well a taper pipe,
Of mold refin'd, becomes his humid lip
Such, such a seat is worthy to receive
The Mystick, *Dionysian*, short cut leaf.
Pandora's box, that angry *Jove* did send,
A fatal troop of Maladies contain'd ;
This better Gift as many cures does hold,
As were diseases in that box of old.
Here, were I not confined in narrow space,
The virtues of the wond'rous herb I'd trace ;
How its green beauties flourished in what ground,
And by what happy chance it was by *Liber* found ;
How the defect of talk it can supply,
If we this other way our breath employ ;
How it collects the thoughts, and serves instead
Of biting nails, or harrowing up the head
But this great task I leave to future rhimes
And abler poets born in better times.

From *Poetical Miscellanies.*   Published by Mr. Steele.
London.   Jacob Tonson, 1714.

POEMS ON THE CIGAR.

SOME sigh for this and that ;
 My wishes don't go far ;
 The world may wag at will,
 So I have my cigar.

Some fret themselves to death
 With Whig and Tory jar,
 I don't care which is in,
 So I have my cigar.

Sir John requests my vote.
 And so does Mr. Marr ;
 I don't care how it goes,
 So I have my cigar.

Some want a German row,
 Some wish a Russian war,
 I care not—I'm at peace,
 So I have my cigar.

I never see the *Post*,
 I seldom read the *Star ;*
 The Globe I scarcely heed,
 So I have my cigar.

They tell me that Bank stock
 Is sunk much under par ;
 It's all the same to me,
 So I have my cigar.

Honours have come to men
 My juniors at the Bar ;
 No matter—I can wait,
 So I have my cigar.

Ambition frets me not,
    A cab or glory's car
    Are just the same to me,
    So I have my cigar.

I worship no vain gods,
    But serve the household Lar,
    I'm sure to be at home,
    So I have my cigar.

I do not seek for fame,
    A General with a scar;
    A private let me be,
    So I have my cigar.

To have my choice among
    . The toys of life's bazaar,
    The deuce may take them all,
    So I have my cigar.

Some minds are often tost
    By tempests like a tar;
    I always seem in port
    So I have my cigar.

The ardent flame of love
    My bosom cannot char,
    I smoke, but do not burn,
    So I have my cigar.

They tell me Nancy Low
    Has married Mr. Parr;
    The Jilt! but I can live,
    So I have my cigar.

THOMAS HOOD.

The Cigar Song.

The sky it was dark, and the way it was long,
   When I mounted his Majesty's Mail ;
And I tried to chirrup a cheery song
   In the teeth of the wind and the hail ;—
But it wouldn t do—so on night's dark face
   I said there should glitter *one* star ;
And I took from snug sleep in its own cozy case,
   And lit up into life a cigar.

And then, as its sweet breath came forth with good-will,
   The sky didn't look half so gruff ;
'Till I felt like a player or poet, who still
   Gets more happy at every puff.
And said I to myself, since mere vapour thus soothes,
   Why should men their bliss ever mar ?
Life's cold spots it warms, and its rough places smoothes,
   And each pleasure is but a cigar !

But—like Hope, self-consuming before its own fire—
   It silently wasted away ;
And I was too happy to stop to inquire
   If there was such a thing as decay.
It was gone ! and I could not another one light !
   But the lesson in love's stronger far ;
Ere the embers of one flame have ceased to be bright,
   Light another—just like a cigar !

From *The Chameleon*, published anonymously by Longmans, Rees & Co., London, 1833. Ascribed to T. Atkinson.

The Smokers.

Smoke, do you ?   Well, then, sir, you know
How fast and firm these habits grow ;

You've often doubtless sworn to quit,
And then forgot it till you'd lit
A fresh cigar, and caught the smell
Of that which pleases you so well.

You've doubtless looked into your purse
And counted cost with many a curse,
And read of dread diseases caught
By smoking oftener than you ought ;
And vowed at least that you'd curtail
The cost and danger, but to fail.

You buy two where 'twas six before—
But go more often to the store ;
You storm and reason with yourself,
And put your box back on the shelf,
But, in whatever place you are.
Your thoughts are with your shelved cigar.

How weak this proves strong men to be !
Free, yet in hopeless slavery !
The thought is madness to the mind ;
We'll burst these galling chains that bind !
But, ere, my friend, we go too far,
I'll thank you for a fresh cigar.

The Columbus Dispatch.

To my Cigar.

(Translated from the German of Friedrich Marc.)

THE warmth of thy glow,
   Well lighted cigar
Makes happy thoughts flow,
   And drives sorrow afar.

The stronger the wind blows
   The brighter thou burnest,
The dreariest of life's woes
   Less gloomy thou turnest.

As I feel on my lip
   Thy unselfish kiss,
Like thy flame colour'd tip,
   All is rosy-hued bliss.

No longer does sorrow,
   Lay weight on my heart,
And all fears of the morrow
   In joy dreams depart.

Sweet cheerer of sadness
   Life's own happy star !
I greet thee with gladness
   My precious cigar !

HIS FIRST CIGAR.

A small boy puffed at a big cigar
   His eyes bulged out and his cheeks sank in :
He gulped rank fumes with his lips ajar,
   While muscles shook in his youthful chin.
His gills were green, but he smole a smile ;
He sat high up on the farmyard stile,
And cocked his hat o'er his glassy eye,
Then wunk a wink at a cow near by.

The earth swam round, but the stile stood still,
   The trees rose up and the kid crawled down

He groaned aloud for he felt so ill,
　　And knew that cigar had "done him brown."
His head was light, and his feet like lead,
His cheeks grew white as a linen spread,
While he weakly gasped, as he gazed afar,
"If I live, this here's my last cigar."

MY LAST CIGAR.

THE mighty Thebes, and Babylon the great,
　　Imperial Rome, in turn, have bowed to fate;
So this great world, and each particular star,
　　Must all burn out, like you, my last cigar:
A puff—a transient fire, that ends in smoke,
　　And all that's given to man—that bitter joke—
Youth, Hope, and Love, three whiffs of passing zest
　　Then come the ashes, and the long, long rest.

From *Nicotiana*, by Henry James Meller.　London.
Effingham Wilson.　1832.

ODE TO MY CIGAR.

YES, social friend, I love thee well.
　　In learned doctors' spite;
Thy clouds all other clouds dispel,
　　And lap me in delight.

What though they tell, with phizzes long,
　　My years are sooner passed?
I would reply, with reason strong.
　　"They're sweeter while they last."

And oft, mild friend, to me, thou art
   A monitor, though still ;
Thou speak'st a lesson to my heart,
   Beyond the preacher's skill.

Thou'rt like the man of worth who gives
   To goodness every day,
The odour of whose virtues lives
   When he has passed away.

When in the lonely evening hour,
   Attended but by thee,
O'er history's varied page I pore,
   Man's fate in thine I see.

Oft, as thy snowy column grows,
   Then breaks and falls away,
I trace how mighty realms thus rose,
   Thus trembled to decay.

Awhile, like thee, earth's masters burn,
   And smoke and fume around,
And then like thee to ashes turn
   And mingle with the ground.

Life's but a leaf adroitly rolled,
   And time's the wasting breath,
That late or early we behold
   Gives all to dusky death.

From beggar's frieze to monarch's robe
   One common doom is passed ;
Sweet nature's work, the swelling globe,
   Must all burn out at last.

And what is he who smokes thee now?
   A little moving heap,

That soon like thee to fate must bow,
   With thee in dust must sleep.

But though thy ashes downward go,
   Thy essence rolls on high ;
Thus, when my body must lie low,
   My soul shall cleave the sky.

                      CHARLES SPRAGUE.

From *The New York Tobacco Plant.*

BOUQUET DE CIGARE.

" My favourite perfume," dear Jennie ?
   Had you asked me an hour ago,
I am sure I'd have lazily answered,
   " My darling, I really don't know."

For I've flirted with many a fragrance,
   And never been constant to one,
But welcomed the roses of summer
   When the dainty spring blossoms were gone.

I find it quite hard to be partial ;
   Most delicious the whole of them are ;
So I'll leave you the sweet smelling flowers—
   My choice is " bouquet de cigare."

That note that was brought me this morning
   (How it made my heart flutter and thrill !)—
Well, the scent of the weed he'd been smoking
   As he wrote it was clinging there still.

And as I read on, dear, it mingled
   With words, oh ! so welcome to me :

He loves me ! he loves me ! and, Jennie,
   Next summer a bridemaid you'll be.

How you stare !—Your blue eyes full of wonder ;
   Yet it may be the day isn't far
When for you too, the perfume of perfumes
   Will be, dear, " bouquet de cigare ! "

Harper's Weekly.

LIFE AND A CIGAR.

" SIR, I know that life's a failure."
   " Early yet to say that, Frank ;
You are young, and not bad-looking,
   Thumping balance in your bank.
Learning, honour, friendship, fortune,
   Love above you like a star,
Sunny skies and dainty dishes,
   When you like, a good cigar."

" Pshaw ! I've been all through the programme,
   Know the thing from first to last ;
All our very brightest pleasures
   Are with shadows overcast,
I have had some mournful moments,
   But I think the saddest far
Was when I found life and loving
   Scarcely worth a good cigar."

Sighed the young and splendid cynic ;
   While his friend said scornfully :
" There's a sadder moment, youngster,
   Yet perchance to come to thee !

F

When life, love, and hope are valued
  At a good cigar—'tis sad ;
But how comfortless the trouble,
  If that good cigar were *bad !* ''

Puck. (New York.) February 25, 1880.

SOUVENIRS OF MY FIRST CIGAR.

'TWAS just behind the woodshed,
  One glorious summer day,
Far o'er the hills the sinking sun
  Pursued its westward way.

And in my one seclusion,
  Safely removed afar
From all of earth's confusion,
  I smoked my first cigar.

Ah, bright the boyish fancies
  Wrapped in the wreaths of blue ;
My eyes grew dim, my head was light,
  The woodshed round me flew.

Dark night closed in around me,
  Rayless without a star,
Grim death, I thought had found me,
And spoiled my first cigar.

I heard my father's smothered laugh,
  It seemed so strange and far ;
I knew he knew, I knew he knew
  I'd smoked my first cigar.

From *The Burlington Hawkeye.*

My First Cigar.

As the years vanish, darling.
   Time, with the sponge of Fate,
Wipes the events we cherish
   Cleanly from Memory's slate ;
E'en the first pair of * *
   That I put on, I vow,
I have forgot their colour,
   Their cut. and their pattern now ;
When did the dawning whisker
   Sprout on my boyish face ?
When did my soaring treble
   Change to a manly bass ?
I have forgotten, darling,
   I have forgotten—but, ah !
One memory ever will haunt me—
   The taste of my First Cigar !

Not in fair Cuba, darling,
   Under a sun of gold ;
Or down in old Virginny
   Were those brown leaves enrolled,
But from the English cabbage
   Sprang the enchanting weed
In a Whitechapel cellar,
   Moulded and made, indeed ;
I cannot tell you, darling,
   How my heart thrill d with glee,
As down on the shiny counter
   Planked I my last two *d.*,
And the fair girl who served me,
   Lounging behind the bar,
Handed across the beer-pulls
   A light for my First Cigar.

F 2

Moments of dire upheaval,
   Darling, your boy has known,
When salmon for supper unsettled
   Sadly his system's tone,
When at two a.m. on the doorstep
   He has stood, with a vacant smile,
Two bob and a toothpick in pocket,
   And wearing a stranger's tile,—
And oft on the billowy ocean,
   His anguish has naught assuaged,
When there was a run on the brandy,
   And the basins were all engaged,—
But even these pangs, my darling,
   Are not to be held on a par
With the writhe, and the rack, and the riot,
   That followed my First Cigar.

                        CLO. GRAVES.

From *Hood's Comic Annual*, 1889.

CONFESSION OF A CIGAR-SMOKER.

I owe to smoking, more or less,
   Through life the whole of my success ;
With my cigar I'm sage and wise—
   Without, I'm dull as cloudy skies.
When smoking all my ideas soar,
   When not, they sink upon the floor.
The greatest men have all been smokers,
   And so were all the greatest jokers.
Then ye who'd bid adieu to care,
   Come here and smoke it into air !

—————:o:—————

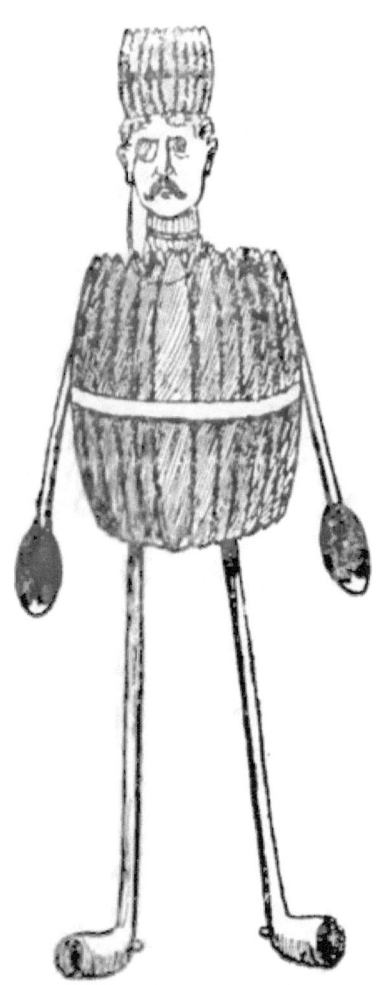

"He is a good liberall Gentleman, he hath bestowed an ounce of Tobacco upon us, and as long as it lasts, come cut and long-taile, weele spend it as liberally for his sake."

ACT IV. SCENE I.

The Returne from Parnassus. Acted at St. John's College, Cambridge, January, 1602.

ON THE CIGARETTE.

I SING the song of the cigarette,
The nineteenth century dudelet's pet ;
   With its dainty white overcoat,
   Prithee, now, make a note,
How your affections entangled get.
The Machiavelian power I sing,
Of the stealthy, insidious, treacherous thing.

What odours unpleasant our nostrils fret !
That subtle aroma we ne'er forget.
   But wherefore complain of it ?
   Spite of the pain of it,
We, too, indulge in our cigarette.
The skeletonizing power I sing,
Of the mind-paralyzing, perfidious thing.

Shades of the past, that linger yet !
Is there no land where laws beset
   Those who lay sense aside,
   Puffing slow suicide,
Into themselves from a cigarette ?
Thither I'd fly, and for ever sing
The praise of the land that is free from the thing.

From the various gamins the slums beget
To the gilded youth with the coronet,
   All of them play with it,
   Seemingly gay with it,
Taking slow death through a cigarette.
The invasive, intrusive, odoriferous thing
Its power autocratic I sadly sing.

What sinner without and beyond the pale
Of civilization, began to inhale,
   Sealing his own sad fate,
   Telling us, oh, too late!
Gibbering lunacy ends the tale.
Husky my voice, I must cease to sing,
I'm puffing, myself, at the poisonous thing.

The Judge.

A DEAD SET AT THE CIGARETTE.

"The note of alarm which has been sounded in the lay
press as to the supposed baneful effects of cigarette smoking
would hardly, we imagine, have found any echo, except in
the silly season."—*Medical Paper.*

So, my white little cigarette,
   Strong language at you they are using ;
And over the doctors' dead set
   At yourself, I am quietly musing.

One morning last week you awoke,
   Like Byron, to find yourself famous —
Let us hope the attack is all " smoke,"
   The assailant a wild ignoramus.

I have loved you a little too well !—
   When in the declension of *"puer,"*
I was led through your nicotine spell
   To be "doctored," as they now say *you* are.

They state that your place in the *case*
   Is to stop there—let this not appal you ;
But they brand you as brutal and base—
   The last plague of Egypt they call you.

Yet somehow the stupid old world
   Goes smoking you, *sans* rhyme or reason ;
For it knows the invective is hurled
   To fill up this dull, silly season.

Judy.   September, 12, 1888.

THE CIGARETTE,

I AM only a small cigarette,
But my work I will get in, you bet,
   For the stern coffin maker
   And grim Undertaker.
Will declare I bring fish to their net.

NO SMOKING ALLOWED.

A Plaintive Song.

THE poets have sung about women and wine,
But smoke is the theme of this ditty of mine ;
I look on my pipe as a trusty old friend,
Who's faithful whatever luck fortune may send.
Wherever I travel, north, east, west, or south,
I've always a pipe or cigar in my mouth,
For when I am smoking I'm up in a cloud,
But, of course, never go where no smoking's allow'd.
     No smoking allow'd, what a terrible sell,
     When they put out my pipe, I am put out as well.

One day by express on the Great Eastern line,
I started to visit an old friend of mine,
I'd lighted my pipe, and was watching the curl
Of the smoke. when there popp'd in a pretty young girl.
I cried "Smoking carriage," the train was just off,
Of course I could not make the dear creature cough.
So put down my pipe and submissively bow'd
To my fate, which I felt was " No smoking allowed."
     No smoking allowed, &c.

I looked at the ceiling, I fear, with a frown,
I looked at the lady, of course she looked down ;
I offered the paper, of the weather I spoke,
And talked about steam though I thought about smoke.
So charming a damsel I'd ne'er seen before,
But soon I admired her fifty times more ;
One small remark proved she with sense was endow'd,
She said, "Go on smoking, sir, smoking's allowed."
     No smoking allowed, &c.

In comfort the rest of the journey was passed,
I'd met with a sensible woman at last !
And now we are married, I oft say in joke,
Our joys and our sorrows have ended in smoke.
She knows that those ladies who smoke cannot bear,
Have husbands who take pipes and glasses elsewhere ;
So ladies pray try to get used to a cloud,
And don't join the cry of " No smoking allowed."
     No smoking allowed, &c,

     :o:

NOTICE OF A NEW SONG.

(In E flat, F flatter, G flattest.)

"The Mixture as Before."

By the Composer of "Expectorate no more;" "From his Nose came the Fairy Cloud;" "One Puff he gave, &c.

This is the finest effort of this world-renowned Composer's magnificent genius.

1st Verse.

A frantic youth,
  With wayward feet,
Walked up and down
  A quiet street,
Ah, sad was he ;
  All hope was gone ;
His cheeks were wild,
  His eye was wan.

This very first movement exhibits the composer's power. The faded numbers on the street doors, and the broken asphalte on the side-walk start suddenly into view. Then, by a repetition of staccato C's, a miraculous representation of a runaway knock is presented to the mind's eye. A dreamy under-current suggests quite plainly a Policeman, with a half-pint behind a convenient waggon.

2nd Verse.

Swift as a thought
  A maiden flies,
A world of joy
  In her brown eyes.
"Oh, love," he yelled,
  "You have, I hope,
The mixture brought,
  Composed by Cope."

The spontaneous gush of joy-bell melody that enters with the flying maiden, lights the scene with tender half-toned hues, and then climbs into resplendent and rose-golden melody. The trembling, extatic, half-hoping, half-fearing yell, too, contains as much as is sometimes found in a whole cantata.

3rd Verse.

Her open hand
A packet shows,
The which the youth
Pops to his nose :
And now they both
Triumphant roar—
"It is the Mix-
Ture as before."

For depth of pathos, height of sublimity, and generous breadth of treatment, this last verse is simply marvellous. The "Mixture as before" will be in the mouths of every one ere long.—Wild Oscar, in the *Bond Street Oracle.*

From *Cope's Tobacco Plant.*

SNUFF: AN INSPIRATION.

THE pungent, nose-refreshing weed,
Which, whether pulverised it gain
A speedy passage to the brain,
Or, whether touched with fire, it rise
In circling eddies to the skies,
Does thought more quicken and refine
Than all the breath of all the Nine.

WILLIAM COWPER.

SGANARELLE, *tenant une tabatière* :—

" Quoi que puissent dire Aristote et toute la philosophie,
il n'est rien d'égal au tabac ; c'est la passion des honnêtes
gens, et qui vit sans tabac n'est pas digne de vivre. Non
seulement il réjouit et purge les cerveaux humains, mais
encore il instruit les âmes à la vertu, et l'on apprend avec
lui à devenir honnête homme. Ne voyez-vous pas bien,
dès qu'on en prend, de quelle manière obligeante on en use
avec tout le monde, et comme on est ravi d'en donner à
droite et à gauche, par-tout où l'on se trouve ? On
n'attend pas même que l'on en demande, et l'on court au-
devant du souhait des gens : tant il est vrai que le tabac
inspire des sentiments d'honneur et de vertu à tous ceux
qui en prennent."

MOLIERE. *Don Juan.* (1665.)

SIX REASONS FOR TAKING SNUFF.

WHEN strong perfumes and noisome scents,
  The suffering nose invade
Snuff, best of Indian weeds, presents
  Its salutary aid.

When vapours swim before the eyes,
　And cloud the dizzy brain,
Snuff, to dispel the mist, applies
　Its quick enlivening grain.

When pensively we sit or walk,
　Each social friend away,
Snuff best supplies the want of talk,
　And cheers the lonely day.

The hand, like alabaster fair,
　The diamond's sparkling pride,
Can ne'er so gracefully appear,
　If snuff should be denied.

E'en Commerce, name of sweetest sound
　To every British ear,
Must suffering droop, should snuff be found
　Unworthy of our care.

For ev'ry pinch of snuff we take
　Helps trade in some degree ;
As smallest drops of water make
　The vast unbounded sea.

Read's *Weekly Journal*.　February 21, 1761.

J'AI DU BON TABAC.

J'AI du bon tabac dans ma tabatière,
J'ai du bon tabac, tu n'en auras pas.
　J'en ai du fin et du rapé,
　Ce n'est pour ton fichu nez.
J'ai du bon tabac dans ma tabatière,
J'ai du bon tabac, tu n'en auras pas.

Ce refrain connu que chantait mon père,
A ce seul couplet il était borné.
    Moi, je me suis determiné
    A le grossir comme mon nez.
J'ai du bon tabac dans ma tabatière,
J'ai du bon tabac, tu n'en auras pas.

Un noble heritier de gentilhommière,
Recueille tout seul un fief blasonné,
    Il dit a son frère puiné
    Sois abbé, je suis ton ainé.
J'ai du bon tabac dans ma tabatière,
J'ai du bon tabac, tu n'en auras pas.

Un vieil usurier, expert en affaire,
Auquel par besoin on est amené,
    A l'emprunteur infortuné,
    Dit, après l'avoir ruiné :
J'ai du bon tabac, dans ma tabatière,
J'ai du bon tabac, tu n'en auras pas.

Juges, avocats, entr'ouvrant leurs serres,
Au pauvre plaideur par eux rançonné,
    Après avoir pateliné,
    Disent, le procés terminé :
J'ai du bon tabac, dans ma tabatière,
J'ai du bon tabac, tu n'en auras pas.

D'un gros financier, la coquette flaire
Le beau bijou d'or de diamants orné.
    Ce grigou, d'un air renfrogné,
    Lui dit : Malgré ton joli nez—
J'ai du bon tabac dans ma tabatière,
J'ai du bon tabac, tu n'en auras pas.

Tel qui veut nier l'esprit de Voltaire,
Est pour le sentir trop enchifrené.

Cet esprit est trop raffiné,
Et lui passe devant le nez.
Voltaire a l'esprit dans sa tabatière,
Et du bon tabac, tu n'en auras pas.

Voilà huit couplets, cela ne fait guère,
Pour un tel sujet bien assaisonné ;
Mais j'ai peur qu'un priseur mal né,
Me chante, en me riant au nez :
J'ai du bon tabac dans ma tabatière
J'ai du bon tabac, tu n'en auras pas.

GABRIEL CHARLES DE LATTEIGNANT (1697-1779.)

A PINCH OF SNUFF

Oh SNUFF ! our fashionable end and aim !
Strasburgh, Rappee, Dutch, Scotch ! whate'er thy name ;
Powder celestial ! quintessence divine !
New joys entrance my soul, while thou art mine.
Who takes—who takes thee not ? where'er I range
I smell thy sweets from Pall Mall to the 'Change.
By thee assisted, Ladies kill the day,
And breathe their scandal freely o'er their tea ;
Nor less they prize thy virtues when in bed,
One pinch of thee revives the vapour'd head.
Removes the spleen, removes the qualmish fit,
And gives a brisker turn to female wit,
Warms in the nose, refreshes like the breeze,
Glows in the head, and tickles in the sneeze.
Without it, Tinsel, what would be thy lot ?
What, but to strut neglected, and forgot !
What boots it for thee, to have dipt thy hands
In odours wafted from Arabian lands ?

Ah ! what avails thy scented *solitaire,*
Thy careless swing and pertly tripping air,
The crimson wash, that glows upon thy face,
Thy modish hat, and coat that flames with lace !
In vain thy dress, in vain thy trimmings shine,
If the Parisian snuff box be not thine.
Come to my nose, then, Snuff, nor come alone,
Bring Taste with thee, for taste is all thy own.

From *The Shrubs of Farnassus*, by J. Copywell.   1760.

THE SNUFF-TAKER.

(By the Rev. W. King, of Mallow, 1788.)

"——Before I budge an inch
I hail Aurora with a pinch ;
After three cups of morning tea
A pinch most grateful is to me ;
If then by chance the post arrive,
My fingers still the deeper dive.
When gallant Nelson gains his point,
I sink in deep to middle joint ;
And soon as e'er the work he clinches,
Oh, then I take the pinch of pinches !
But if our heroes chance to fail,
I seldom go beyond the nail.
If I on ancient classics pore,
Or turn their learned pages o'er,
I take a pinch at every pause,
A tribute of my just applause,
Whene'er I dip in page historic,
Or pass an hour in wit with Yorick,
I relish more each paragraph
If season'd with a pinch and laugh.

G

Or if discussing subjects curious,
I revel in a pinch luxurious ;
E'en joyous friends and claret rosy,
Insipid are *sans* pinches cosy.
Whate'er I do, where'er I be,
My social box attends on me ;
It warms my nose in winter's snow,
Refreshes midst midsummer's glow ;
Of hunger sharp it blunts the edge,
And softens grief, as some allege.
Thus, eased of care or any stir,
I broach my freshest canister ;
And freed from trouble, grief, or panic,
I pinch away in snuff balsamic ;
For rich or poor, in peace or strife,
It smoothes the rugged path of life."

———

Epigram on Snuff-taking.

Whatever apes there are of Indian breed,
In apish tricks some people them exceed ;
Witness that odious and indecent fashion
Of smutty snuffy noses in our nation.
When Tonsor hath used all the art he knew,
To smooth, to sweeten, and set out a beau ;
Then straight out comes a box of stinking dust,
'Cause others do bedaub their face, he must.
Cœlia, the fair, both paints and pulves her hair.
And her unseemly parts all covered are ;
Yet open and exposed is one foul place,
Her nose besnuffed—the scandal of her face ;
Yet Cœlia like an angel is adorned—
What whim then cause her make herself deformed ?

Who would pretend a graceful look to prize,
And yet this nasty fashion idolize ?

Written about 100 year ago, when ladies largely indulged
in snuff, and Queen Charlotte was popularly known as
" Snuffy Charlotte," on account of her love for it.

SNUFF.

A DELICATE pinch ! oh how it tingles up
The titillated nose, and fills the eyes
And breast, till in one comfortable sneeze
The full-collected pleasure bursts at last !
Most rare Columbus ! thou shalt be for this
The only Christopher in my calendar.
Why, but for thee the uses of the nose
Were half unknown, and its capacity
Of joy. The summer gale that from the heath,
At midnoon glowing with the golden gorse,
Bears its balsamic odour, but provokes
Not satisfies the sense ; and all the flowers,
That with their unsubstantial fragrance tempt
And disappoint, bloom for so short a space,
That half the year the nostrils would keep Lent,
But that the kind tobacconist admits
No winter in his work ; when Nature sleeps,
His wheels roll on, and still administer
A plentitude of joy, a tangible smell.

What are Peru and those Golcondan mines
To thee, Virginia ? miserable realms,
The produce of inhuman toil, they send
Gold for the greedy, jewels for the vain.
But thine are *common* comforts !—To omit

Pipe-panegyric and tobacco praise,
Think what a general joy the snuff box gives
Europe, and far above Pizarro's name
Write Raleigh in thy records of renown !
Him let the school-boy bless if he behold
His master's box produced, for when he sees
The thumb and finger of authority
Stuffed up the nostrils : when hat, head, and wig
Shake all ; when on the waistcoat black, brown dust,
From the oft-reiterated pinch profuse
Profusely scattered, lodges in its folds,
And part on the magistral table lights,
Part on the open book, soon blown away,
Full surely soon shall then the brow severe
Relax ; and from vituperative lips
Words that of birch remind not, sounds of praise,
And jokes that *must* be laughed at shall proceed.

ROBERT SOUTHEY. *Poet Laureate.*

The Eccentric Snuff-taker.

SHOULD trade be dull, and times go rough,
Oh ! give me then a pinch of snuff ;
Give me my box a pinch to take,
E'en when I'm pleased for pleasure's sake.
When fortune's frowns disturb my mind,
And friends appear to grow unkind,
Relief I seek within my box,
My system is quite orthodox.
When a true friend perchance I meet
I cheerfully his person greet,
A hearty " how d'ye do ? " takes place,
When lo ! my snuff box shows its face.

My pulveriferous box supplies
A recipe for weakly eyes ;
That man must be a silly goose
Who thoughtlessly condemns its use.
If my proboscis could but speak,
'Twould often say the dose repeat :
Each grateful sneeze and titillation
Excites a frequent iteration,
Then here's my glass, in which I toast
Success to that which I love most,
Reader, I pray, don't think me bluff—
Mark well the hint !—'tis *Grimstone's Snuff.*

An advertisement by Mr. W. Grimstone, 39, Broad
Street, Bloomsbury, dated June, 1840.

SNEEZING.

WHAT a moment, what a doubt !
All my nose is inside out,—
All my thrilling, tickling caustic,
Pyramid rhinocerostic,
Wants to sneeze and cannot do it !
How it yearns me, thrills me, stings me,.
How with rapturous torment wrings me !
Now says, "Sneeze, you fool,—get through it."
Shee—shee—oh ! 'tis most del—ishi—
Ishi—ishi—most del—ishi !
(Hang it, I shall sneeze till spring !)
Snuff is a delicious thing.

LEIGH HUNT.

Two Ways of Sneezing.

When you take a pinch of snuff,
If you but inhale enough,
You'll produce exacerbations
Of excessive sternutations
With opisthotonic flexions,
Virtually in all directions.
And as sure as this the case is
Cyanotic angiectasis
Will ensue, with dialysis—
Which you may, or mayn't, think nice is.
Ere you, though, can play the critic,
Lesions dacryocystitic
Lead to what, in fact, the close is—
Lacrymal apocenosis !

*   *   *   *

'Stead of this, though, if you please,
You can take the snuff and—*Sneeze.*

To my Nose.

Knows he that never took a pinch,
Nosey, the pleasure thence which flows !
    Knows he the titillating joys
    Which my nose knows ?
O nose ! I am as proud of thee
As any mountain of its snows ;
I gaze on thee, and feel that pride
    A Roman knows ?

ALFRED CROWQUILL.

The Comic Offering. 1834.

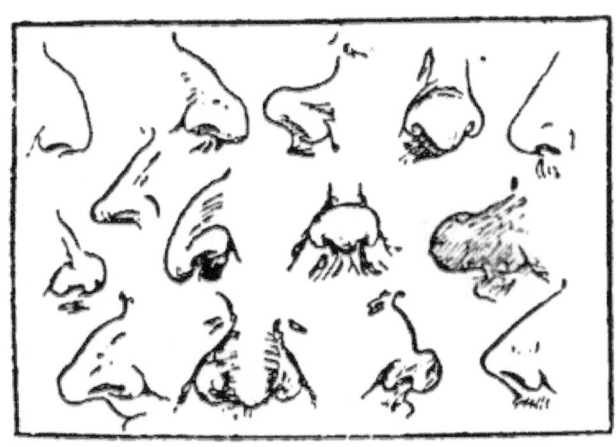

PARODIES ON SMOKING.

One of the earliest burlesque poems in praise of Tobacco was that written by Mr. Isaac Hawkins Browne about one hundred and fifty years ago, entitled "*A Pipe of Tobacco*, in imitation of Six Several Authors."

This poem has been repeatedly reprinted, although there is little in it that strikes a modern reader as either remarkably humorous or clever. The authors imitated are Colley Cibber (the Poet Laureate), Ambrose Phillips, James Thomson, Edward Young, Alexander Pope, and Jonathan Swift, Dean of St. Patrick's. It is stated that the imitation of Ambrose Phillips was not written by Mr. I. H. Browne, but was sent to him by a friend, whose name has not been transmitted to us. This is to be regretted, as this particular imitation (the second) is generally considered the best in the collection. According to Ritson this was written by Dr. John Hoadley.

A PIPE OF TOBACCO:
In Imitation of Six Several Authors.

IMITATION I.
Laudes egregii Cæsaris————
Culpâ deterere ingeni.

HOR.

A NEW-YEAR'S ODE.
Recitative.

OLD battle-array, big with horror is fled,
And olive-robed peace again lifts up her head.
Sing, ye Muses, Tobacco, the blessing of peace ;
Was ever a nation so blessed as this ?

Air.

When summer suns grow red with heat,
  Tobacco tempers Phœbus' ire,
When wintry storms around us beat,
  Tobacco cheers with gentle fire.
    Yellow autumn, youthful spring,
    In thy praises jointly sing.

Recitativo.

Like Neptune, Cæsar guards Virginian fleets,
  Fraught with Tobacco's balmy sweets ;
Old Ocean trembles at Britannia's pow'r,
  And Boreas is afraid to roar.

Air.

Happy mortal ! he who knows
Pleasure which a Pipe bestows ;
Curling eddies climb the room,
Wafting round a mild perfume.

Recitativo.

Let foreign climes the vine and orange boast,
While wastes of war deform the teeming coast ;
Britannia, distant from each hostile sound,
Enjoys a Pipe, with ease and freedom crown'd ;
E'en restless Faction finds itself most free,
Or if a slave, a slave to Liberty.

Air.

Smiling years that gayly run,
Round the Zodiack with the sun,
Tell, if ever you have seen
Realms so quiet and serene.
Britain's sons no longer now
Hurl the bar, or twang the bow,

Nor of crimson combat think,
But securely smoke and drink.

Chorus

Smiling years that gayly run
Round the Zodiack with the sun,
Tell, if ever you have seen
Realms so quiet and serene.

IMITATION II.

Tenues fugit ceu fumus in auras.

VIRG.

LITTLE tube of mighty pow'r,
Charmer of an idle hour,
Object of my warm desire,
Lip of wax, and eye of fire:
And thy snowy taper waist,
With my finger gently brac'd;
And thy pretty swelling crest,
With my little stopper prest,
And the sweetest bliss of blisses,
Breathing from thy balmy kisses.
Happy thrice, and thrice agen,
Happiest he of happy men;
Who when agen the night returns,
When agen the taper burns;
When agen the cricket's gay,
(Little cricket, full of play)
Can afford his tube to feed
With the fragrant Indian weed:
Pleasure for a nose divine,
Incense of the god of wine.
Happy thrice, and thrice agen,
Happiest he of happy men

IMITATION III.

——— *Prorumpit ad æthera nubem*
Turbine fumantem piceo.

VIRG.

O THOU, matur'd by glad Hesperian suns,
Tobacco, fountain pure of *limpid* [1] *truth*,
That looks the very soul; whence pouring thought
Swarms all the mind; absorpt is yellow care,
And [2] *at each puff imagination burns.*
Flash on thy bard, and with exalting fires
Touch the mysterious lip, that chaunts thy praise
In strains to mortal sons of earth unknown.
Behold an engine, wrought from tawny mines
Of ductile clay, with *plastic* [3] *virtue* form'd,
And glaz'd magnifick o'er, I grasp, I fill.
From *Pætotheke* [4] with pungent pow'rs perfum'd,
Itself [5] *one tortoise all, where shines imbib'd*
Each parent ray; then rudely ram d illume,
With the red touch of zeal-enkindling sheet,
Mark'd [6] *with Gibsonian lore;* forth issue clouds,
Thought-thrilling, thirst-inciting clouds around,
And many-mining fires : I all the while,
Lolling at ease, *inhale* [7] the breezy balm.
But chief, when *Bacchus wont with thee to join*
In genial strife and orthodoxal ale,
Stream [8] *life and joy into the Muses' bowl.*
Oh be thou still *my great inspirer,* thou
My Muse; oh fan me with thy zephyrs boon,
While I, in clouded tabernacle shrin'd,
Burst forth all oracle and mystick song.

---

[1] Poem on Liberty, ver. 12.   [2] Ibid. ver. 16.   [3] Ibid.
ver. 104.   [4] A poetical word for a Tobacco-box.
[5] Poem on Liberty, ver. 243, 245.   [6] Poem on Liberty, ver. 247.   [7] Ibid. ver 309.   [8] Ibid. ver 171.

IMITATION IV.

—— *Bullatis mihi nugis,*
Pagina turgescat, dare pondus idonea fumo.

PERS.

CRITICKS avaunt ; Tobacco is my theme ;
Tremble like hornets at the blasting steam.
And you, court-insects, flutter not too near
Its light, nor buzz within the scorching sphere.
Pollio, with flame like thine, my verse inspire,
So shall the Muse from smoke elicit fire.
Coxcombs prefer the tickling sting of snuff ;
Yet all their claim to wisdom is—a puff :
Lord Fopling smokes not—for his teeth afraid :
Sir Tawdry smokes not—for he wears brocade.
Ladies, when pipes are brought, affect to swoon ;
They love no smoke, except the smoke of town ;
But courtiers hate the puffing tribe,—no matter,
Strange if they love the breath that cannot flatter !
Its foes but shew their ignorance ; can he
Who scorns the leaf of knowledge, love the tree ?
The tainted templar (more prodigious yet)
Rails at Tobacco, tho' it makes him—spit.
Citronia vows it has an odious stink ;
She will not smoke (ye gods !) but she will drink :
And chaste Prudella (blame her if you can)
Says, pipes are us'd by that vile creature Man :
Yet crowds remain, who still its worth proclaim,
While some for pleasure smoke, and some for fame :
Fame, of our actions universal spring,
For which we drink, eat, sleep, smoke,—ev'rything.

IMITATION V.

——— *Solis ad ortus*
Vanescit fumus.

LUCAN.

BLEST leaf! whose aromatick gales dispense
To templars modesty, to parsons sense:
So raptur'd priests, at fam'd Dodona's shrine
Drank inspiration from the steam divine.
Poison that cures, a vapour that affords
Content, more solid than the smile of lords:
Rest to the weary, to the hungry food,
The last kind refuge of the wise and good.
Inspir'd by thee, dull cits adjust the scale
Of Europe's peace, when other statesmen fail.
By thee protected, and thy sister, beer,
Poets rejoice, nor think the bailiff near.
Nor less the critick owns thy genial aid,
While supperless he plies the piddling trade.
What tho' to love and soft delights a foe,
By ladies hated, hated by the beau,
Yet social freedom, long to courts unknown,
Fair health, fair truth, and virtue are thy own.
Come to thy poet, come with healing wings,
And let me taste thee unexcis'd by kings.

———

IMITATION VI.

Ex fumo dare lucem.

HOR.

BOY! bring an ounce of Freeman's best,
And bid the vicar be my guest:
Let all be placed in manner due,

A pot wherein to spit or spue,
And *London Journal* and *Free Briton,*
Of use to light a pipe————

    *   *   *   *

This village, unmolested yet
By troopers, shall be my retreat :
Who cannot flatter, bribe, betray ;
Who cannot write or vote for pay.
Far from the vermin of the town,
Here let me rather live, my own,
Doze o'er a pipe, whose vapour bland
In sweet oblivion lulls the land ;
Of all which at Vienna passes,
As ignorant as ———— Brass is :
And scorning rascals to caress,
Extoll the days of good Queen Bess,
When first TOBACCO blest our isle,
Then think of other Queens—and smile.

Come jovial pipe, and bring along
Midnight revelry and song ;
The merry catch, the madrigal,
That echoes sweet in City Hall ;
The parson's pun, the smutty tale
Of country justice o'er his ale.
I ask not what the French are doing,
 Or Spain to compass Britain's ruin :
   Britons, if undone, can go,
   Where TOBACCO loves to grow.

————:o:————

HORACE.

In imitation of Epode III.

AN ODE AGAINST TOBACCO.

FOR parricide, that worst of crimes,
Hemlock's cold draught, in ancient times,
  Scarce taught the rogue repentance :
But had tobacco then been known,
Its burning juices swallow'd down,
  Had prov'd a fitter sentence.

How callous are the lab'rers jaws,
Who this dire weed both smokes and chaws,
  And feasts upon the venom !
While I by chance a taste once got,
That so inflam'd my mouth and throat,
  I thought all hell was in 'em.

Sure, this vile drug, that serv'd me thus,
The deadly viper's poisonous juice
  Infus'd must have great share in ;
Or else some hag, with midnight wish,
Procur'd it as a special dish
  Of Satan's own preparing.

This was the charm Medea taught
Her dear advent'rous Argonaut,
  To steal the Golden Fleece with ;
Down bulls and dragons gaping throat
A quid he threw, which, quick as thought,
  The brutes were laid at peace with.

Ting'd in tobacco's baleful oil,
Her presents made her rival broil

Past Jason's art of quenching :
And when he swore revenge, the witch
Mounted aloft astride her switch,
  Pleas'd she had spoil'd his wenching.

Under the blue I'd rather live,
And the sun's fiercest rays receive,
  How apt soe'er to burn us :
Nay, Hercules's shirt I'd wear,
Or any flame much sooner bear,
  Than a pipe's fiery furnace.

My merry lord, if quid or whiff
You ever taste of this damn'd leaf,
  May you meet with what you dread most,
May Chloe, when with her you lie,
And press to kiss her, put you by,
  And rather hug the bed post !

From *The Gentleman's Magazine.* May, 1744.

————:o:————

HAMLET (?) ON SMOKING.

To smoke or not to smoke, that is the question ?
Whether 'tis worthier, in respect of morals,
To cherish the narcotic as a dainty friend,
Or shun, as dangerous, what some may call
An evil, slavish habit. To smoke ! a luxury,
No more ; and, by a smoke, to say we make
This life the more worth living, and calm
The storm of thought and nerve, 'tis a consummation
Devoutly to be wished. To smoke, to chew,
To snuff, or one or all : ay, there's the rub ;
For, if in use, we do ourselves abuse,

H

And wreck the independence of our will ;
We sure must pause !   There are the effects
Which anti-smokers say tobacco brings ;
For who would smoke, or use in any form,
That which would injure Nature's laws, cause waste
Of precious time and money ; a barrier
Raise betwixt the sexes ; his physical
Constitution undermine.   Servile practice
Make a second self ; when he for all time
Might abjure the pipe?   Who would use the weed
To court and risk those numerous evils,
But that the thought that they are idle cant
Of him who never smoked—a prejudice
More selfish than it seems—puzzles the will,
And makes the smoker rather chance the ills
Than forswear any pleasure that tobacco gives.
Thus conscience does but our discretion crave,
And thus our resolution brought to scratch,
We claim—our nature's great prerogative—
The right to use in moderation wise all things ;
With this regard, that we do none offend,
But gently use our liberty.

SMOKESPEARE.

From *The Cigar and Tobacco World.*   March 15, 1889.
This is a monthly journal of the Tobacco Trade, ably
edited by Mr. P. H. Davis.   Although it was only started
last January, it has already taken a leading position, owing
to its useful information, and its humorous articles and
illustrations.

HAMLET'S SOLILOQUY ON TOBACCO.

To SMOKE or not to smoke, that is the question :
Whether a mild cigar assists digestion ;

Or, whether it begets a kind of quaintness,
Which some would say was nothing but a faintness ;
To smoke—to drink and then to go to bed ;
To find a pillow for an aching head ;
To snore—perchance to dream ! and half your senses scare
With visionary demons or nightmare ;
To wake, in perspiration nicely dished,
'Tis a consummation hardly to be wished ;
For who would bear the kicks, cuffs, and abuse
Of this base world, when he might cook his goose
Upon his toasting fork ? Or who would care
For half the motley groups which at him stare,
Some morning early, stuck before the bench,
When soda-water would his fever quench,
But that a little thing within doth call ?
Thus porter doth make rumuns of us all !
And thus our resolution to keep sober
Is drown'd and soon forgot in good October.
But hush ! my Phelia comes, the pretty dear !
Oh ! think of me love—when you fetch your beer.

ANONYMOUS.

TO SMOKE, OR NOT TO SMOKE.

To smoke, or not to smoke—that is the question !
Whether 'tis better to abjure the habit,
And trust the warnings of a scribbling doctor,
Or buy at once a box of best Havanas,
And ten a day consume them ? To smoke, to puff,
Nay more, to waste the tender fabric of the lungs
And risk consumption and its thousand ills
The practice leads to—'tis a consummation
Discreetly to be shunned. To smoke, to puff—

To puff, perhaps to doze—ay, there's the rub ;
For in that dozing state we thirsty grow,
And, having burned the tube up to a stump,
We must have drink, and that's one cause
We modern youth are destined to short life ;
For who can bear to feel his mouth parched up,
His throat like whalebone and his chest exhausted,
His head turned giddy, and his nerves unstrung,
When he himself might drench these ills away
With wine or brandy?   Who could live in smoke,
And pine and sicken with a secret poison ;
But that the dread of breaking o'er a rule
Prescribed by Fashion, whose controlling will
None disobey, puzzles ambitious youth,
And makes us rather bear the ills we feel
Than others that the doctor warns us of.
Thus custom does make spectres of us all,
And thus the native hue of our complexion
If sicklied o'er with a consumptive cast ;
The appetite, a loss of greater moment,
Palled by the weed, and the digestive powers
Lose all their action.

JOHN W. FARRELL.

Rare Bits.   November 18, 1882.

AN IMITATION OF MR. ABRAHAM COWLEY.

"THE lazy Earth doth steam amain,
And fumes and smokes beneath the rain :
The Rivers, Brooks, and Rivulets are
No less in smoke particular
At nightfall : and the storm blast loud

Is often wont to *blow a cloud*
Around the mountain-tops, and they
Do take delight in this same way ;
And send a fiery fume from out
Their angry heights, and such a rout
Of burnt-up *ashes,* that do strow
Great cities in the plains below.
The *setting Sun* is oft made dim
With smoky mists that circle him.
So all the World's on *smoking* bent,
And puffs and fumes to its content :
Fill up the bowl then, fill it high,
Fill all the gaping pipes, for why
Should every creature smoke but I :
Why, man of morals, tell me why ? ''

From " *The Anatomy of Tobacco :* or Smoking Methodised,
Divided, and Considered after a New Fashion." By Leolinus
Siluriensis. London. George Redway, 1884.

———:o:———

Elegy.

Written over an old Pipe-Box.

The postman hits his last rat-tat to day,
   And hies him to his lowly home with glee ;
My wife reposes in her white array ;
   The night is left to " 'Bacca " and to me.

Now starts a glimmering bottle on the sight,
   And all the air a spirit perfume holds ;
At sight of me the cockroach takes to flight,
   And leaves awhile my common dips and moulds.

All raving now, at yonder area gate,
   The moping " bobbies " to the cooks complain
That soldiers, with their padded breasts elate,
   Molest their ancient privilege and reign.

Beneath this hingeless lid, bound round with braid,
   Wherein no anti-vermin dare to creep
(Each one done brown, aside for ever laid),
   The ancient tutors of my smoking sleep.

The bull-like voice of nicotinian Bob,
   The sylph-like tones of sweet, poetic, Ned,
The fierce denouncings of the anti-mob,
   No more shall call them from their narrow bed.

For them no more the fierce fusee shall burn,
   Or plugs be purchased and put in with care ;
In memory only, I to them return ;
   Their smoke, too strong, would all my nerves impair.

Oft have they lain with me in some green field ;
   Their solace oft some stiff-neck'd care has broke.
How strangely sorrow to the pipe doth yield,
   And joy descends e'en through ascending smoke.

Let not philosophy at smoking mock—
   Philosophy is but its prototype ;
Nor e'en religion hear with spurning shock,
   The short and simple annals of the pipe.

     *   *   *   *

Ah me ! In this neglected box is laid
   Old pipes, once glowing with the scented fire ;

Pipes for which shillings, ay, and pounds were paid.
  Start not—'tis true, or I'm a living liar !

But pipes on pipes of " Bacca," day by day,
  With poison laden, did their fates control ;
Strong-smelling oil stopp'd up the narrow way,
  And now they may no more console my soul.

Full many a pipe, of purest briar root,
  The stern schoolmaster confiscates and breaks ;
Full many a clay, too, seized is by the brute,
  And flung with tops and marbles, buttons, cakes.

One colour'd meerschaum that, in hidden poke
  Conceal'd, full many a day in school did lie,
Escaped the notice of the stern-eyed bloke,
  To linger in this box and never die.

To take excursion by the iron way,
  In smoking-carriage, where thick clouds arise ;
To fumigate—(tho' anti-smokers brav),
  And blow their ashes into people's eyes—

Their state forbids. Now, circumscribed they lie,
  For pleasure useless, and for work as well ;
Weak, helpless, all, I bid them now good-by ;
  For, tho' so weak, dear me, how strong they smell !

For thee, who, brooding thus with bended head,
  Deploring much their sad and helpless state,
If chance, by nicotinian feelings led,
  Some brother smoker shall inquire thy fate :

Haply some wooden-headed clown may say :
  " I've often seed him, when the ale-house closed,

Wandering along the all-too narrow way,
  His eyes a quiver, like to one who dozed ;

"There, at the foot of yonder painted sign,
  That looks more like a pig than like a cow,
He'd drink his beer—it would'nt run to wine—
  And smoke his pipe, all reckless—anyhow.

"Or down the street, to put his watch in pawn,
  Feeling for vanish'd coppers, he would rove,
His old hat on, his bristly chin unshorn.
  He liked his beer, but warn't a drunken cove.

"One night I miss'd him at the accustom'd pub ;
  Unoccupied remain'd his favourite seat.
Another came. Where was he ?—sore the rub ;
  In losing him, we lost a look'd-for treat.

"The next, with solemn march, in blue array
  (A crowd behind with strong tumultuous din,)
Two bobbies came. They'd found him on the way,
  With beer o'ercome, and so they ran him in ! "

THE EPITAPH.

Here rests, with his old head upon a stone,
  A man who smoked till he did reason drown.
To-morrow morn the mayor, all fully blown,
  Will frown on him, and fine him half-a-crown.

H. L.

From *Cope's Tobacco Plant.* September, 1874.

———— :o: ————

A Song, after Sheridan.

HERE's to the hookah with snake of five feet,
  Or the " portable " fix'd to one's " topper " ;
Here's to the meerschaum more naughty than neat,
  And here's to all pipes that are proper.
        Fill them up tight,
        Give 'em a light ;
  I'll wager a smoke will set everything right.

Here's to the Warden's twelve inches of stalk,
  Here's to Jack Tar's clay, with one, sir ;
To the pipes now with mountings so rich that they " walk,"
  And here's to most pipes which have none, sir.
                Fill them up tight, &c.

Here's to the Milo just out of the shop,
  With mouthpiece as dry as pale sherry ;
Here's to your veteran, wet as a mop,
  Black as a sloe or a cherry.
                Fill them up tight, &c.

Let them be clumsy, or let them be slim,
  Light or heavy, I care not a feather ;
So, fill them with 'Baccy right up to the rim,
  And let us all smoke them together.
        Fill them up tight,
        Give 'em a light ;
  I'll wager a smoke will set everything right.

From *Cope's Tobacco Plant.*   February, 1875.

———:o:———

HAIL TO THE PLANT.

(A Parody of Sir Walter Scott.)

HAIL! to the Plant which we owe to brave Raleigh,
  Long may it flourish on Cuba's lone shore,
Bloom on the mountain, and spread in the valley,
  Fertile, and fragrant, and fresh evermore !
        Bright sunshine, nourish it,
        Gentle deeds, cherish it,
Life giving breezes, around it still flow ;
        Moisture and warmth, give aid,
        That it may never fade ;
Tabak, St. Nicotine, ho, ieroe !

      *   *   *   *

Smoke, brother, smoke of the pride of Virginia ;
  Snuff, brother, snuff, if you'd clear up your brain ;
Chew, brother, chew, and I'll bet you a guinea,
  Once fairly started, you'll do it again.
        Oh, would our northern air
        Nurture this plant so rare !
Never aught else in my garden I'd grow :
        All my flowers pluck'd should be,
        Fruit-trees give place to thee,
Tabak, St. Nicotine, ho, ieroe !

THE LAY OF THE LAST SMOKER.

THE weed was rank, the pipe was old,
Along the road the smoker rolled ;
His scared and hesitating way
Showed that he owed and couldn't pay.
The pipe, his one remaining joy,

Was scoff of every man and boy ;
For last of all the smokers, he,
This old man was well known to be.
For 'Bacca's day was lately fled,
And all his brother smokers dead ;
And he but stayed to smoke and swear,
And wonder where the others were.
No more amid the jest and song,
He puffed at his churchwarden long ;
No longer in a smoking car
He blew a cloud from his cigar,
And stood his ground both stern and stout,
To smoke the anti-puffers out.
Old days were drowned in Time's dark stream,
And "antis" reigned now all supreme ;
The quivering noses of the time
Now called each harmless puff a crime.
A wandering smoker, scorned and sad,
He nearly drove the city mad ;
And had to smoke—oh ! wretched elf !
Some 'Bacca that he grew himself.

*   *   *   *

From *Cope's Tobacco Plant.* April, 1876.

———: o: ———

THE LAST CIGAR.

(After Thomas Moore.)

'TIS a last choice Havana
    I hold here alone ;
All its fragrant companions
    In perfume have flown.

No more of its kindred
    To gladden the eye,
So my empty cigar case
    I close with a sigh.

I'll not leave thee, thou lone one,
    To pine ; but the stem
I'll bite off and light thee
    To waft thee to them,
And gently I'll scatter
    The ashes you shed,
As your soul joins its mates in
    A cloud overhead.

All pleasure is fleeting,
    It blooms to decay
From the weeds glowing circle,
    The ash drops away.
A last whiff is taken,
    The butt-end is thrown,
And with empty cigar case
    I sit all alone.

———

'Tis the last weed of Hudson's
    Left lying alone ;
All his dark brown Regalias
    Are vanished and gone.
No cigar of its colour,
    No " Lopez " is mine,
To delight with its perfume
    And fragrance divine.

I'll not leave thee, thou lone one !
    I'll ring for a light ;

Thy companions are ashes,
    I'll smoke thee to-night.
Thy halo and incense
    Shall rise o'er my head,
As I sigh for the beauties
    All scentless and dead.

And soon may I follow
    Those lov'd ones' decay ;
Since from each tempting bundle
    They've faded away.
When Regalias are smok'd out,
    And " Lopez " are blown,
Oh ! who would still linger,
    Cigarless, alone ?

From *Hints to Freshmen, in the University of Oxford.*
By Canon Hole. Oxford. J. Vincent.

A Last Cigar.

'Tis my last mild Havana
    Pervading the room ;
Her companions have taken
    Their *leaves* in a fume.
No kindred *to back her,*
    Nor plug, twist, nor snuff,
To return her aroma
    Or give puff for puff.

Oh, fain would I follow
    When the last whiff is sped,
And in life's brightest garden
    The *weeds* are all dead.

When troubles oppress us,
    Or better-halves jar,
Oh, what were existence
    Without a cigar?

————:o:————

THE BUTCHER BOY.

THE butcher boy down the road has gone,
With beefsteak he has lined him ;
A pipe of clay he has put on,
And his basket's slung behind him.
    "Lend me that," cried the baker's boy,
    "The pipe you now are biting,"
"Not I," cried he, "my pipe I'll guard!"
    And so they fell to fighting.

The butcher fell, but the baker's boy,
Could not bring his proud soul under ;
The pipe he loved ne'er smoked again,
For he broke its stem asunder ;
    And cried, "No dough shall sully thee,
    I'll be thy undertaker ;
Thy joys were made for the butcher boy—
    Thou shalt ne'er be smoked by a baker!"

                                        H. L.

From *Cope's Tobacco Plant*.   July, 1873.

————

MY OLD DHUDEEN.

(Air : *Love's Young Dream*.)

OH ! the days are gone when lollipops
        My heart could move ;
When sugar-sticks and almond rock

Were my first love ;
Inventions sweet
And succulent,
Made childhood all serene ;
Now there's nothing half so sweet in life
As my old Dhudeen ;
Yes, there's nothing half so sweet in life
As my old Dhudeen.

For the youth will tire at last of sweets
When " down " appears,
And he wears a collar in the streets
That hides his ears :
The vile " Pickwick "
May make him sick,
And turn his face quite green,
Yet there's nothing half so sweet in life
As his old Dhudeen ;
Oh ! there's nothing half so sweet in life
As his old Dhudeen.

Oh ! the first sly smoke I'll ne'er forget—
It made me queer ;
And when I my stern parent met,
He pulled my ear ;
But now I'm old,
And weak and cold,
And on my stick do lean,
There's nothing half so sweet in life
As my old Dhudeen ;
Oh ! there's nothing half so sweet in life
As my old Dhudeen.

H. L.

From *Cope's Tobacco Plant.* December, 1872.

I Remember.

(*After Thomas Hood.*)

I REMEMBER, I remember,
  The pipe that first I drew ;
With red waxed end and snowy bowl,
  It perfect was and new.
It measured just four inches long,
  'Twas made of porous clay ;
I found when I began to smoke,
  It took my breath away,

I remember, I remember,
  In fear I struck a light ;
And when I smoked a little time,
  I felt my cheeks grow white.
My nervous system mutinied,
  My diaphragm uprose,
And I was very—very ill
  In a way you may suppose.

I remember, I remember,
  The very rod he got,
When father who discovered me,
  Made me exceeding hot.
He scattered all my feathers then,
  While, face down I reclined ;
I sat upon a cold hearthstone,
  I was so warm behind.

I remember, I remember,
  I viewed the rod with dread,
And silent, sad, and supperless,
  I bundled off to bed.

It was a childish punishment,
   And now 'tis little joy
To know that, for the self-same crime,
   I wallop my own boy !

From *Cope's Tobacco Plant.*   March, 1875.

————: o :————

The Old Black Clay.

I LOVE it ! I love it ! though some may say
It's wrong to be fond of an old black clay ;
I haven't exactly inlaid it with sighs—
The turn of my mind has been otherwise—
For I always feel excessively gay
When I'm gazing upon that old black clay.

When rude and frivolous folk are by,
I never produce it—I'll tell you why--
They call it harsh, injurious names,
And vex my soul with mischievous games ;
But when to a lonely place I repair,
I make quite sure there's nobody there,
And adore in the most abandoned way
That stumpy loveable coal-black clay.

I'll never forget the dreadful day
When they " played it low " on that harmless clay—
The ruthless hand of a mother dear
Hid it away in a dust-hole drear ;
But, ah ! no words can properly tell
My joy when I found it again by the smell ;
And I took to my heart (as one may say),
Once more that redolent, long lost clay.

I

I love it! I love it! as I have said,
I smoke it abroad, and I smoke it abed ;
And if the prophecy turn out right
That I'm burned to a cinder some fine night,
I'll simply deem it a glorious way
Of ending my life with my faithful clay.

The Manchester City Jackdaw. April 21, 1876.

———:o:———

SMOKE NOT!

SMOKE not, smoke not your weeds nor pipes of clay
Cigars that are made from leaves of cauliflowers ;—
Things that are doomed no duty e'er to pay ;—
Grown, made, and smokèd in a few short hours.
　　　　　　　　Smoke not, smoke not.

Smoke not, smoke not! the weed you smoke may chang
The healthfulness of your stomachic tone ;
Things to the eye grow queer and passing strange ;
All thought seems undefined—save one, to be alone.
　　　　　　　　Smoke not, smoke not.

Smoke not! the tradesman whose weed you smoke may
　　die!
May perish from the cabbage-bearing earth ;—
The sordid *dun* into your chamber hie—
Sent by the trustees in their tinless dearth.
　　　　　　　　Smoke not, smoke not.

Smoke not, smoke not! O, warning vainly said!
Cane and cap-paper since we first did try,

Smoke flings a halo round the smoker's head ;
And all in vain do anxious mothers cry,
Smoke not, smoke not !

From *Hints to Freshmen in the University of Oxford*,
published by J. Vincent, Oxford, and attributed to the Rev.
Canon Hole.

———:o:———

THE PIPES OF ENGLAND.

THE stately pipes of England,
   How beautiful they be,
With amber tips and meerschaum bowls—
   Such pipes are not for me !
With scented Latakia they burn,
   And golden crowns they wear ;
And the smoke steals from the scented urn—
   Like summer's perfumed air.

The merry pipes of England,
   Amid the joke and jest,
With gladsome glasses of hot grog,
   Are found then at their best,
The smoker's eye is seen to wink,
   As many a tale is told ;
Or lips ope cheerfully to drink
   The glorious ale of old.

The cottage pipes of England—
   By thousands made of clay—
All snowy in their wooden box,
   How beautiful are they !

From ruddy lips they outward poke,
　　As white as wool or lard ;
And the lowly do a cheerful smoke,
　　When the times are not too hard.

The free, fair pipes of England
　　Live long in hall and hut ;
And sweet for ever be their lips,
　　And scented be their bowls ;
And may no humbug e'er eclipse
　　The solace of our souls.

From *Cope's Tobacco Plant.*　April 1873.

————:o:————

The Genius of Smoking.

[*We have been favored with the following defence of
smoking, by an intimate literary friend of Lord Byron,
who assures us it is selected from several unpublished juve-
nile trifles written at various times in his album by the
noble bard.*]

I HAD a dream—it was not all a dream ;
Methought I sat beneath the silver beam
Of the sweet moon, and you were with me there,
And everything around was free and fair ;
And from our mouths upcurled the fragrant smoke,
Whose light blue wreaths can all our pleasures yoke,
In sweetest union to young Fancy's car,
And waft the soul out thro' a good cigar.
There as we sat and puffed the hours away,
And talked and laughed about life's little day,
And built our golden castles in the air,
And sighed to think what transient things they were,

As the light smoke around our heads was thrown,
Amidst its folds a little figure shone,
An elfin sprite, who held within her hand
A small cigar her sceptre of command.
Her hair above her brow was twisted tight off,
Like a cigar's end, which you must bite off ;
Her eyes were red and twinkling like the light
Of Eastern Hookah, or Meerschaum, by night ;
A green tobacco leaf her shoulders graced,
And dried tobacco hung about her waist ;
Her voice breathed softly, like the easy puffing
Of an old smoker, after he's been stuffing.
Thus as she rolled aside the wanton smoke,
To us, her awe-struck votaries she spoke,—
" Hail faithful slaves ! my choicest joys descend
On him who joins the smoker to the friend,
Yours is a pleasure that shall never vanish
Provided that you smoke the best of Spanish ;
Puff forth your clouds "—(with that we puff'd amain)
" Sweet is their fragrance "—(then we puff'd again)
" How have I hung, with most intense delight,
Over your heads when you have smoked at night,
And gratefully imparted all my powers
To bless and consecrate those happy hours ;
Smoke on," she said.   I started and awoke,
And with my dream she vanished into smoke.

ANONYMOUS.

——:o:——

AN AMERICAN PARODY OF WORDSWORTH'S "SONNET ON THE SONNET."

SCORN not the meerschaum. Housewives, you have
croaked

In ignorance of its charms.   Through this small reed
Did Milton, now and then, consume the weed;
The poet Tennyson hath oft evoked
The Muse with glowing pipe, and Thackeray joked
    And wrote and sang in nicotinian mood ;
    Hawthorne with this hath cheered his solitude ;
A thousand times this pipe hath Lowell smoked ;
Full oft hath Aldrich, Stoddard, Taylor, Cranch,
    And many more whose verses float about,
        Puffed the Virginian or Havanna leaf;
And when the poet's or the artist's branch,
    Drops no sustaining fruit, how sweet to pout
        Consolatory whiffs—alas, too brief!

———— :o: ————

My Hookah.

WHAT is it, that affords such joys
On Indian shores, and never cloys,
But makes that *pretty, bubbling* noise ?
                    My Hookah.

What is it, that a party if in
At breakfast, dinner, or at Tiffin,
Surprises and delights the Griffin ?
                    My Hookah.

What is it to Cadets gives pleasure?
What is it occupies their leisure ?
What do they deem the greatest treasure ?
                    My Hookah.

Say—what makes Decency wear sable?
What makes each would-be nabob able
To cock his legs upon the table?
                    My Hookah.

What is it (trust me, I'm not joking,
'Tis truth—altho', I own, provcking)
That sets e'en Indian *belles* a smoking?
My Hookah.

What is it—wheresoe'er we search
In ev'ry place ;—*except the Church,*
That leaves sweet converse in the lurch?
My Hookah.

But hold my Muse—for shame for shame—
One question ere you smoking blame—
What is it gives your book a name?
My Hookah.

My fault I own—my censure ends ;
Nay more—I'll try to make amends,
Who is the *safest* of all friends?
My Hookah.

Say who ? or what retains the power,
When fickle Fortune 'gins to lour,
To solace many a lonely hour ?
My Hookah.

When death-like dews and fogs prevailing
In Pinnace or in Budg'-row sailing,
What is it that prevents our ailing ?
My Hookah.

When we're our skins with claret soaking,
And heedless wits their friends are joking,
Which friend will stand the *greatest smoking?*
My Hookah.

By what—(nay, answer at your ease,
While pocketing our six rupees)—
By what d'ye mean the town to please?

> My Hookah.

From MY HOOKAH; or, *The Stranger in Calcutta.* Being a collection of Poems by an Officer. Calcutta: Greenway. and Co., 1812.

A PINCH OF SNUFF.

WITH mind or body sore distrest,
Or with repeated cares opprest,
What sets the aching heart at rest?

> A pinch of snuff!

Or should some sharp and gnawing pain
Creep round the noddle of the brain,
What puts all things to rights again?

> A pinch of snuff!

When speech and tongue together fail,
What helps old ladies in their tale,
And adds fresh canvass to their sail?

> A pinch of snuff!

Or when some drowsy parson prays,
Or still more drowsy people gaze,
What opes their eyelids with amaze?

> A pinch of snuff!

A comfort which they can't forsake,
What is it some would rather take,
Than good roast beef, or rich plum cake?

> A pinch of snuff

What warms without a conflagration,
Excites without intoxication,
And rouses without irritation ?
>> A pinch of snuff !

Then let us sing in praise of snuff !
And call it not such "horrid stuff,"
At which some frown, and others puff,
>> And seem to flinch

But when a friend presents a box,
Avoid the scruples and the shocks
Of him who laughs and her who mocks,
>> And take a pinch !

From *The Sportsman.* August, 1835.

STANZAS TO A LADY

In defence of Smoking.

WHAT taught me first sweet peace to blend
With hopes and fears that knew no end,
My dearest, truest, fondest friend ?
>> My pipe, love !

What cheer'd me in my boyhood's hour,
When first I felt Love's witching power,
To bear deceit,—false woman's dow'r
>> My pipe, love !

What still upheld me since the guile,
Attendant on false friendship's smile,
And I in hope, deceiv'd the while ?
>> My pipe, love !

What cheer'd me when misfortunes came,
And all had flown me? Still the same
My only true and constant flame,
My pipe, love!

What sooth'd me in a foreign land,
And charm'd me with its influence bland,
Still whisp'ring comfort, hand in hand?
My pipe, love!

What charm'd me in the thoughts of past
When mem'ry's gleam my eyes o'ercast,
And burns to serve me to the last?
My pipe, love!

Nicotiana, by H. J. Meller. London. E. Wilson, 1832.

To my Cigar.

WHEN cares oppress the drooping mind,
And fickle friends are most unkind,
Who constant still remains behind?
My true cigar!

Oh! where's the friend who'd cheerfully,
To soothe one pensive hour for me,
Resign his latest breath like thee—
My kind cigar?

Thy spirit's gone, poor fragile thing!
But still thine ashes, mouldering,
To me a valued lesson bring,—
My pale cigar!

Like man's, how soon thy vital spark,
Expiring, leaves no other mark,
But mouldering ashes, drear and dark,
    My dead cigar.

       T. G. J.

Bristol. 1844.

TOBACCO.

WHENE'R I'm out of sorts or sad,
Oppress'd with care, and well-nigh mad,
What comforts me, and makes me glad?
    Tobacco !

What builds such castles in the air,
And paints my prospects bright and fair,
And makes me negligent of care ?
    Tobacco !

How is it that I'm so resign'd,
When'er my wife *must* speak her mind,
And ne'er retaliate in kind ?
    Tobacco !

What makes my holidays so sweet,
And ev'ry "outing" such a treat
That I would fain their joys repeat ?
    Tobacco !

Whene'er my brain is dull and dark,
And utterly beside the mark,
What wakes the latent, slumb'ring spark ?
    Tobacco !

What changes all my scowls to smiles,
And many a tedious hour beguiles,
And ne'er by any chance me riles,

                    Tobacco.

Enlarger of our mortal ken,
Familiar of the artist's den,
Beloved by literary men—

                    Tobacco !

Far kinder than the kindest friend,
O, teach us how your powers blend !
And from your heavenly throne descend,
                    Tobacco !

                              E. H. S.

From *Cope's Tobacco Plant.*   April, 1873.

———

The Weed.

When roses droop beside the wall,
When lily petals fade and fall,
What swiftly rises, covering all?
                    The Weed.

When starts the widow on the chase,
To fill "the late lamented's" place,
What decorates her pretty face ?
                    The Weed.

When coffee's served and wine runs low,
When conversation waxes slow,
What brings the after-dinner glow ?
                    The Weed.

A Smoke.

WHAT comforts me when I am sad,
Or when I've got the toothache *bad*,
Or when the money market's mad?
                              A smoke.

What soothes me if I dine not well,
When lies about me people tell,
Or friendship proves a hollow sell?
                              A smoke.

What quiets indigestion's pangs,
And takes the edge off hatred's fangs,
And salves misfortune's cruel bangs?
                              A smoke.

———:o:———

HYMN TO SAINT NICOTINE.

(Imitation of Dr. Oliver Wendell Holmes.)

STRANGE ! that this gently breathèd cloud
  So far, far sweeter unto me,
Than all that this green earth enshroud,
  Or float above the sea.
My meerschaum, when thy mouth I greet,
  No lady's lips seem half so sweet.

I look upon the fair blue skies,
  And naught but empty air I see ;
But when thy circling cloudlets rise,
  It seemeth unto me
Ten thousand angels spread their wings,
  Within those little azure rings.

Tobacco hath the choicest leaf
  That ever western breeze hath fanned ;
Its healing odour gives relief
  To men of ev'ry land.
This precious herb to me doth yield
  More joy than all the broider'd field.

O, comrade ! there be many things
  That seem right fair in truth or joke ;
But sure from none among them springs
  A richer charm than smoke.
Let us not puff our pipes alone,
  But join two altars both in one.

From *Cope's Tobacco Plant.*   December, 1871.

———— :o: ————

PARODY OF DR. WATTS, BY AN ANTI-SMOKER.

How doth the nasty, dirty man,
  Go smoking every hour ;
And spend his money wastefully
  On Old Nick's favourite flower.

How wistfully he seeks his pipe,
  How glad he doth it light ;
And smokes the foul thing all the day,
  And feels quite ill at night.

In shag, bird's eye, or honey-dew,
  His mind is ever fast ;
And Satan knows to him he's due,
  For he'll get him at last.

THE LAST PIPE.

T'WAS the voice of the doctor, I heard him declare,
"You've been smoking too much, of tobacco beware!
To be candid and plain you'll find it no joke,
For you'll become *ashes* yourself if you smoke."

So I've filled my last pipe as I sit by the fire,
And gaze at the cloud rising higher and higher,
And languidly watching each up-curling ring,
A mournful adieu to tobacco I sing.

Farewell, good cigars, I will e'en call you dear,
Yet your price were no object so you were still here.
Good bye! Latakia, Mild Turkey, good by!
Virginia, Cavendish, Bristol Bird's-eye,

And my pipe! My sweet pipe, with thy cool amber tip!
No more shall that amber caress my fond lip.
Oh! friend of my youth! must thou really go—
My partner in joy, and my solace in woe?

'Tis too true; nought avail me these heart-broken sighs!
And, alas! thou art out.   There are tears in my eyes,
As I lay thee down gently.   I will not complain,
But I feel I shall never be happy again.

Fun, 1870.

————:o:————

THE PIPE.

A Parody of Barry Cornwall's "*The Sea, the Sea!*"

THE pipe, the pipe, the German pipe!
The short, the long, the meerschaum ripe!
Its odorous puffs without a sound,

They float my head's wide regions round;
They rise in clouds and mock the skies,
While *Baccy* snugly cradled lies.
My hookah wide! my hookah deep!
I've that which I would ever keep;
With the smoke above, and smoke below,
And smoke wheresoe'er I go.
If a storm (like a Chinese gong) should ring
    What matters that? I'll smoke and sing.
        What matters, &c.

I love—oh! how I love to smoke,
And drink full bumpers of th' foaming soak!
And when its waves have drowned my soul,
I'll whistle aloud such a "Tol-de-rol!"
Don't ask me where the world is going,
Nor why the sou'-west *blast* is blowing.
I never breathed the dull tame air,
But I relish my great pipe mair and mair,
And back again flew for a soothing puff,
Like a bird—I'm sure that's quick enough.
My *mother* it is, and I'll prove it to ye,
(Much more of a mother than the open sea!)
For *smoking*, I'm at it ever and ever!
I hope your comment on this line is "clever!"
For fear of growing at all lackadaisical
I hasten to lay down my pen *parody*-sical;
In truth these stanzas concluding with somewhat
'Bout "birth" and "death," which things I can't come
I've only one word, and that's to crave pardon,
These sweet pretty verses that I've been so hard on.

From *The Individual.* Cambridge, January 31, 1837.

————:o:————

A Dream (Anti-cipated.).

(After Kingsley.)

Three Antis* went groaning out into the east—
   Out into the east, as the sun arose ;
Each thought on the newspaper he loved the least ;
   The *Tobacco Plant* followed, and chaff'd at their woes.
But antis will croak, and smokers will smoke,
Tho' chaff it be sudden, and endless the joke
      That the antis afford with their moaning.

The *Plant* having stopped in a garden bower,
   Lit up his sweet pipe, as the sun arose ;
And he heard those three antis bawl out by the hour
   The weakest of humbug, in seedy old clothes.
But antis will croak, and the *Plant* have his joke,
And chaff, if ignited, must all end in smoke,
      And the antis must soon end their moaning.

Three antis lay drunk on the shining sands,
   In the morning gleam, as the sun arose ;
And smokers are laughing and rubbing their hands,
   To know they're already relieved of their foes.
For *Observers* will talk, and the *Plant* doesn't sleep ;
Though tough be the job, 'tis amusing to keep
      All the anti-Tobaccoites moaning.

From *Cope's Tobacco Plant.* January, 1875.

---

* *Antis i.e.,* Anti-smokers.

K

ODE TO TOBACCO.

THOU who, when fears attack,
Bidst them avaunt, and Black
Care, at the horseman's back
      Perching, unseatest ;
Sweet when the morn is grey ;
Sweet, when they've clear'd away
Lunch ; and at close of day
      Possibly sweetest :

I have a liking old
For thee, though manifold
Stories, I know, are told,
      Not to thy credit ;
How one (or two at most)
Drops make a cat a ghost—
Useless, except to roast—
      Doctors have said it :

How they who use fusees
All grow by slow degrees
Brainless as chimpanzees,
      Meagre as lizards ;
Go mad, and beat their wives ;
Plunge (after shocking lives)
Razors and carving knives
      Into their gizzards.

Confound such knavish tricks !
Yet know I five or six
Smokers who freely mix
      Still with their neighbours ;
Jones—(who, I'm glad to say,

Asked leave of Mrs. J—)
Daily absorbs a clay
   After his labours.

Cats may have had their goose
Cooked by tobacco-juice ;
Still why deny its use
   Thoughtfully taken ?
We're not as tabbies are :
Smith, take a fresh cigar !
Jones, the tobacco-jar !
   Here's to thee, Bacon !

     C. S. CALVERLEY.

<hr />

DETAINED.

HAND me another spill—
Phœbe, my glass refill,
As I've some time to kill.
   What do you mention ?
Boat, gun, and tackle nigh,
Horse and trap ready ?—I
Think I can manage my
   Task of detention.

Rowing ? I've had a bout !
Raining ? Then can't go out !
Capital stream for trout ?
   Not very handy !
No, I'll just pen a lay ;
Clear all these things away ;
Landlord ! another clay,
   Soda and brandy

Anti-Tobaccoite !
I have no wish to fight
But if you douse my light,
        Mind, we shall wrangle.
Why should you interfere,
With your new-fangled gear,
And try *my* course to steer
        At such an angle ?

No ! I must have my light ;
Whether I read or write,
Smoking, by day or night,
        Aids the reflection.
Some may prefer Bohea ;
Excellent though it be,
I think Tobacco the
        Pink of Perfection !

Shag's my divinity,
Pure as virginity ;
In its vicinity
        Come not, you croakers !
What, though the *Antis* choke ?
Still I must have my smoke ;
Pshaw ! let the beggars *croak !*
        Here's to the smokers !

                      E. H. S.

————:o:————

BEWARE !

I KNOW a meerschaum fair to see,
        Take care !
It whispers " Smoke and colour me,"

Beware ! beware !
Smoke it not,
'Tis fooling thee !

It cost two guineas, golden brown,
    Take care !
You'd better smash it ; drop it down ;
    Beware ! beware !
    Smoke it not ;
    'Tis fooling thee.

A mouthpiece of a golden hue,
    Take care !
'Twill very likely make you—vomit,
    Beware ! beware !
    Smoke it not !
    'Tis fooling thee.

It hath a bowl as white as snow,
    Take care !
Smoke it black, to Old Nick you'll go ;
    Beware ! beware !
    Smoke it not ;
    'Tis fooling thee.

                          P. C.

TOBACCO SMOKE !

THE clouds of smoke were rising fast,
As through a college room there passed
A youth, who bore, 'spite sage advice,
A "baccy"-pouch, with strange device,
            "Tobacco smoke ! "

His brow was sad ; his eye beneath
Glared on a pipe, laid in its sheath,
And in his ears there ever rung
The accents of the donor's tongue,
            Tobacco smoke !

In ground-floor rooms he saw the light,
Of pipes and weeds glow strong and bright ;
And, heedless of the passing don,
From out his lips escaped a groan,
            Tobacco smoke !

"Try not the shag," the old man said,
"It is o'er strong for thy young head,
Dire its effects to those untried ; "
Heedless he was, and but replied,
            Tobacco smoke !

"Oh, stay," the maiden said, and test
Our Latakia—'tis the best !"
He grasped his packet of birds'-eye,
And only muttered with a sigh,
            Tobacco smoke !

"Beware ; don't set your room alight—
The college might object—good night ! "
Such were the words the scholar spoke,
And scarcely heard through closing oak,
            Tobacco smoke !

At midnight hour, as bedroom-ward
Two "undergrads" from drinking hard,
Steered up the gas-less break-neck stair,
A voice cried from the "right two-pair,"
            Tobacco smoke !

The Freshman by his scout was found,
Lying all prone upon the ground,
And still his hand grasped like a vice
The " baccy "-pouch with strange device,
      Tobacco smoke !

There, in the morning cold and gray,
Moaning, and all unkempt, he lay,
And then the scout, unmoved, serene—
Said—" Oh ! 'tis easy to be seen,
      Tobacco smoke ! "

           R. C.

From *College Rhymes.* Part XVI., 1864.

 The Song of Firewater, a parody of Longfellow's " Song
of Hiawatha," appeared in *Cope's Tobacco Plant* for
November, 1871. The poem relates to snuff, but as it
extends to over 200 lines it cannot be inserted here. It
commences thus :—

   SHOULD you ask me whence this story ?
   Whence this legend and tradition ?
   I should answer, I should tell you,
   From the lips of Blow-me-tite-o ;
   Blow-me-tite-o, sweetest singer,
   Singer of the mournful ditties.

  *   *   *   *

The Song of Nicotine.

SHOULD you ask me why this meerschaum,
Why these clay-pipes and churchwardens,
With the odours of tobacco,
With the oil and fume of "mixture,"
With the curling smoke of "bird's eye,"
With the gurgling of rank juices,
With renewed expectorations
As of sickness on the fore-deck?
   I should answer, I should tell you,
From the cabbage, and the dust-heaps,
From the old leeks of the Welshland,
From the soil of kitchen gardens,
From the mud of London sewers,
From the garden-plots and churchyards,
Where the linnet and cock-sparrow
Feed upon the weeds and groundsel,
I receive them as I buy them
From the boxes of Havana,
The concoctor, the weird wizard.
   Should you ask how this Havana
Made cigars so strong and soothing,
Made the "bird's eye," and "York-river,"
I should answer, I should tell you,
In the purlieus of the cities,
In the cellars of the warehouse,
In the dampness of the dungeon,
Lie the rotten weeds that serve him
In the gutters and the sewers,
In the melancholy alleys,
Half-clad Arab boys collect them,
Crossing-sweepers bring them to him,
Costermongers keep them for him,
And he turns them by his magic

Into "cavendish" and "bird's-eye,"
For those clay-pipes and churchwardens,
For this meerschaum, or he folds them,
And "cigars" he duly labels
On the box in which he sells them.

From *Figaro.* October 7, 1874.

LINES TO THE "ANTI-TOBACCO JOURNAL."

TELL me not in penny numbers
    Smoking's but a loathsome dream;
Worse than onions and cucumbers,
    Though they be chawed up like steam !

Smoke is sweetness, done in earnest,
    Power possessing to console,
If 'tis healthy weed thou burnest
    In the clay or meerschaum bowl.

Not to aid expectoration
    Doth the smoker burn the weed,
But to woo sweet meditation,
    And also digest his "feed."

"Shag" is strong, "Returns" is milder,
    "Cavendish" but suits the brave ;
Though our pulses beat the wilder,
    Still for 'bacca do we crave.

In this world so full of brawling,
    If in years your manhood's ripe,
Heed ye not the antis' calling—
    Be a man and smoke a pipe.

Pipes of great men all remind us
   (Tho' of clay the bowl and stem),
Wheresoever fate may find us,
   We can colour pipes like them.

Dhudeens, that perhaps another
   On the wheel of fortune broke,
Some forlorn and bankrupt brother,
   Seeing, may take heart, and smoke.

Let us, then, take weeds and matches,
   And a pipe—that is enough ;
Tho' it only be by snatches,
   Spared from toil, we still will puff !

From *Cope's Tobacco Plant.*   March, 1876.

MEERSCHAUM.

COME to me, O ! my meerschaum,
   For the vile street organs play ;
And the torture they're inflicting
   Will vanish quite away.

I open my study window
   And into the twilight peer,
And my anxious eyes are watching
   For the man with my evening beer.

In one hand is the shining pewter,
   All amber the ale doth glow ;
In t'other are long " churchwardens,"
   As spotless and pure as snow.

Ah ! what would the world be to us
  ·Tobaccoless ?—Fearful bore !
We should dread the day after to-morrow
  Worse than the day before.

As the elephant's trunk to the creature,
  Is the pipe to the man, I trow ;
Useful and meditative
  As the cud to the peaceful cow.

So to the world is smoking ;
  Through that we feel, with bliss,
That, whatever worlds come after,
  A jolly old world is this.

Come to me, O ! my meerschaum,
  And whisper to me here,
If you like me better with coffee
  Than grog, or the bitter beer.

Oh ! what are our biggest winnings
  If peaceful content we miss?
Though fortune may give us an innings,
  She seldoms conveys us bliss.

You're better than all the fortunes
  That ever were made or broke ;
For a penny will always fill you,
  And buy me content with a smoke.

The Pipe and the Quid.

An imitation of Longfellow's " The Arrow and the Song."

I FLUNG a pipe into the air,
And it fell down, I knew not where ;
For many folks were near to me,
And so I did not stay to see.

I spun a quid up in the air,
And that fell down, I knew not where ;
For 'twould require the strongest sight
To follow a quid in its erring flight.

Shortly I found my pipe again,
On the head of my uncle broke in twain ;
And the quid I had not seen descend,
I found in the eye of my dearest friend.

WRONGFELLOW.

Cope's Tobacco Plant.   June, 1876.

———:o:———

Another Match.

(After *A. C. Swinburne.*)

IF love were dhudeen olden,
     And I were like the weed,
Oh ! we would live together,
And love the jolly weather,
And bask in sunshine golden,
     Rare pals of choicest breed ;
If love were dhudeen olden,
     And I were like the weed.

If I were what cigars are,
     And love were like the case,
In double rows or single,
Our varied scents we'd mingle,
Both brown as Persian shahs are—
     (You recollect *his* face) ;
  If I were what cigars are,
     And love were like the case.

If you were snuff, my darling,
     And I, your love, the box,
We'd live and sneeze together,
Shut out from all the weather,
And anti-snuffers snarling,
     In neckties orthodox ;
  If you were snuff, my darling,
     And I, your love, the box.

If you were oil essential,
     And I were nicotine,
We'd hatch up wicked treason,
And spoil each smoker's reason,
Till he grew penitential,
     And turned a bilious green ;
  If you were oil essential,
     And I were nicotine.

If you were shag of dark hue,
     And I were mild bird's eye,
We'd scent the passing hours,
And fumigate the flowers ;
And in the midnight, hark you,
     The Norfolk Howards should die
If you were Shag of dark hue,
     And I were mild Bird's-eye.

If you were the aroma,
 And I were simply smoke,
We'd skyward fly together,
As light as any feather ;
And flying high as Homer,
 His grey old ghost we'd choke ;
If you were the aroma,
 And I were simply smoke.

From *Cope's Tobacco Plant.*   August, 1876.

ANOTHER BALLAD OF MORE BURDENS.

(After Swinburne.)

THE burden of false meerschaums : Fair to sight
Built up by scamps in a most fraudful way,
With glass for amber, can't be seen at night,
But looketh what it is in truthful day.
And bowls that turn (with dirt) to dirty grey,
And narrow bores that all our jaws do tire,
And fill our souls with horrible dismay.
   This is a cause of every smoker's ire.

The burden of bad 'Bacca : This is worse.
A burden with full fruit of mild swearing :
We drop the pipe to sigh a gentle curse,
Six score between the morn and evening.
The quivering of the glands, the shuddering,
The wheezy grunts with which we do respire,
Makes " weed " seem horrid and a treacherous thing.
   This is a cause of every smoker's ire.

The burden of burnt breeches : Nay, sit down ;
Cover thyself and sleep ; for verily
The market women all about the town
Behind thy back shall laugh and hoot at thee.
Like the red beet-root all thy face shall be ;
That box of lights set thy coat tails on fire,
And burnt thee bare.   Tarry till daylight flee.
       This is a cause of every smoker's ire.

The burden of the missus : oh ! her tongue
Shall let thee rest not, e'en upon thy bed ;
For that her curtains at the window hung,
Of stale smoke smelling, fill her soul with dread.
With mutton cold thou shalt be often fed,
And drink cold grog, against thy warm desire,
And wear a broomstick round thy shrinking head.
       This is a cause of every smoker's ire.

The burden of mean cadgers ; thou shalt flee
All ways at once, but still they will be seen ;
And at the thing thou seest thy face shalt be
Transmogrified, and not at all serene.
And thou shalt say of 'Bacca, " It hath been
Consumed by me ; " and they shall whisper "Liar ; "
And go their ways with chagrin turning green.
       This is a cause of every smoker's ire.

The burden of sad Antis : Every day
They will prognosticate thy doom, and tell
Where thou art going to at last, and say
The place is warm and undesirable.
And swear that for a mile thy clothes do smell ;
And preach to thee till thy whole soul doth tire ;
Then, going, groan—just for a parting knell.
       This is a cause of every smoker's ire.

The burden of the taxes : Spoiled is Spring,
With fragrant 'Bacca 'neath the growing trees,
To think of what we pay for this one thing,
The dearest physic for our miseries.
For, at each puff, the weeping smoker sees
His wreath fly up, away, and higher, higher,
Till thoughts of bankruptcy do make him freeze.
         This is a cause of every smoker's ire.

The burden of the fusees : Some won't light,
And some will spit out fire upon the hands ;
The wretch who sells them slinketh in the night,
And counts his fortune in far, foreign lands
Where police are not, and where are no cab-stands,
While we still on his head heap curses dire
And blame the makers of the various brands.
         This is a cause of every smoker's ire.

The burden of fierce headaches : When we must
Forsake the weed, altho' 'tis our delight,
When all our eyes seem red with blinding dust,
And on our head a weight hangs day and night,
And our red faces, lo ! are bloodless white ;
When nothing in the world we do admire,
And folks do ask us when we last were tight.
         This is a cause of every smoker's ire.

L'ENVOY.

Smokers, and ye whom 'Bacca tickleth,
Heed what is here before the weed you fire ;
You cannot smoke for ever. Where's your breath?
         This is a cause of every smoker's ire.

SINBURN.

From *Cope's Tobacco Plant.* September 1876.

THE CIGAR-SMOKERS.

"'Courage!' he said, and pointed towards the land;
'This mounting wave will roll us shoreward soon.'
In the afternoon they came unto a land
In which it seemed always afternoon."

The Lotos Eaters—*Alfred Tennyson.*

I.

"Land ho!" he cried' "I see it now," says he,
"This jolly breeze will fetch us soon to land."
Towards night they got there, time for early tea,
A land where tea seemed ever smoking hot to stand.
Thick clouds of smoke, by sleepy breezes fanned,
Twined, serpent like, o'er all, in curves and twists;
The setting sun glared red and angry, close at hand,
And from his steaming brow fell off the mists,
As falls the sweat from boxers, boxing with their fists.

II.

A land of smokers! smoking fast were some,
Quick, restless puffers wand'ring to and fro;
And some, with drowsy eyes and senses dumb,
Rolled heavy smoke-clouds very long and slow.
The strangers saw the smokers come and go
Along the shore, in groups of eight and sometimes ten,
From somewhere up above to somewhere down below;
Strange, dingy faces, strongly-perfumed men,
Smelling as husbands when their wives ask, where they've
    been.

III.

The sun went out, the moon began to rise,
But could not shine; smoke rests on everything

L

And closes o'er the sea ; the hum of flies
Is heard afar, and vast musquitoes sing,
　　Who buzz and nearer buzz, then 'light and sting ;
A place where all things always sleepy feel !
　　And round about and in and out, on odorous wing,
With faces like an owl, and tail unlike an eel,
The red-eyed ghosts of old Tobacco-smokers steal.

IV.

Great leaves of that disgusting weed they brought,
And some chopped fine to chew, and also snuff,
　　Whereof they gave to each, but who once caught
The taste, from him the strangely-smelling stuff
　　Took all good sense, nor said he ever, " hold ! enough ;"
The ocean's voice he heard as tho' it spake
　　To some one else ; his own grew thick and gruff,
And half asleep and scarcely half awake,
An everlasting puffing, puffing he did make.

V.

They sat them down upon the dingy shore,
Betwixt the moonlight and the moonlight's ray,
　　And closed their eyes with heavy eyelids o'er,
And saw the "old folks' " faces far "at home " away ;
　　But dark and dismal seemed the tossing bay,
Dismal the hammock's swing, the boatswain's cry.
　　Then one man said, " We won't go home, to-day ! "
And all at once chimed in, " Agreed say I ;
Let's all together not go home till by-and-by ! "

CHORIC SONG.
I.

THERE'S sweet tobacco here, of every kind,
Sweeter than honey in the hollow tree,

Or sugar in the sugar-cane, you'll find,
Or dew-drop in the hollyhock can be ;
 Cigars whose smoke floats lightly round the eye,
As round the buttercup the butterfly ;
 Cigars that one would die to smoke, then smoke to die !
Here lie long-nines beside,
And plugs no teeth have ever tried,
And all the earth is snuff too, far and wide,
And in the craggy rocks the cigarettos hide !

II.

Why leave dry land to sail on boiling water ?
Why make our short lives, any longer, shorter
By still debating, while the minutes flee?
All folks smoke here ; why only smoke not we?—
 We who have smoked vile smoke as e'er was known,
And chewed vile chews on land and sea,
 Still from a bad one to a worse one thrown !
Nor ever end our woes,
By snuffing up the nose,
 Nor yield our senses to the potent spell ;
Nor hearken to the song that o'er us goes ;
 " No joy that tongue can tell
Is like what enters thro' the avenue of smell ! "

III.

 Hateful is the pea-green sky,
Hanging o'er the pea-green sea—
 Life ends in smoke, oh ! why
Should life all labor be ?
 Let us alone. We do not want to go !
Since life's a vapor, smoke it all away !
 Let us alone. We have no strength to row,

We won't attempt it, anyhow, to-day.
Let us alone.   What fun can sailors find
In climbing up a wave, and down behind?
All folks have rest excepting only tars,
Their work is always of the endless kind ;—
Give us a smoke or sleep, sound sleep or good cigars !

IV.

How sweet it were, seeing the rising fog,
With half-cigar and half a smile,
Dozing in a half-and-half the while,
To dream and dream like yonder aged frog,
Which only leaves his hole, the smoky log,
To muse amid abandoned stumps near by ;
Chewing Tobacco, here to lie
And see the waves rush up, our joy to share,
Clutching with eager arms the vacant air,
To grasp the sweets the scented breezes bear ;
To give our minds up to it wholly,
To chase away blue-thoughted melancholy,
To put rich flavorous, antique fine-cut tobacco,
Into these pipes by steady use grown blacker ;
Pressed down with thumb to make it stay ;
Two pinches of black dust shut in a bowl of clay.

V.

Our wives and children are at home, 'tis true ;
But we can do without them, I and you ;
All things have undergone a change back there ;
Our babes climb other knees ; our shirts new husbands
        wear !
They would not know us now, so dirty grown :
So strong we smell they'd slam the angry door,

Thinking our souls upon the wings of smoke had flown,
Been puffed away upon this dingy shore,
Leaving behind the wasted stumps alone,
Fit on the ash-pile only to be thrown.
Let what is, be as 'tis, of course ;
A wife is hard to reconcile ;
We might be driven out by force ;
'Tis hard to fix things, when they've run awhile ;
'Twould be at best our labor for our pains ;
He gains but little who a woman gains :
Sad work, for hearts worn out with household noise,
And arms grown lame long since with nursing baby-boys !

VI.

Tobacco-posies blossom high and low ;
Tobacco-posies bloom where'er you go ;
All day the breezes from the ocean dipping,
O'er hill and vale, on tireless tiptoe tripping,
Up and down the sandy beach the dust of the Tobacco
    blow.
We have done enough of rolling and of pitching, O !
Up the foremast, up the hindmast, in the musty hold below,
While the bellowing boatswain shouted his eternal " Yo
    heave ho ! "
Let us take an oath and keep it, with an open eye,
In the land of the Tobacco still to live and lie,
On the bank, like pigs together, you and also I ;
For they lie beside each other, and the slops are hurled
All around them in the gutter, while their tails are tightly
    curled
All around them—glad and happy, in a glad and happy
    world;
There they smile in comfort, dreaming over future joys

Dreading neither thirst nor hunger, sun nor storm, nor
    roaring noise,
Swearing men, nor scolding women, barking dogs, nor
    tyrant boys.
But they smile, they smell a prospect of a dinner by-
    and-bye,
Steaming up, a preparation making in the kitchens nigh,
And their tail is full of meaning when it's curled so high !
But the luckless race of human labor for their life,
Plant and dig and raise potatoes, mostly keep a wife ;
Wife who scolds them late and early, more than one would
    think,
'Till they lose their senses nearly—some, 'tis whispered, take
    to drink—
Swigging endless potions—others in Tobacco islands dwell,
Resting weary legs, at last, on beds of assfoodel.
Surely, surely, smoking is more nice than not—the chew,
Than life upon the great big ocean, with so much work to
    do ;
Oh ! bless you, brothers, yes of course, we'll stay here, I
    and you !

    This is taken from a small volume of American parodies,
entitled "*The Song of Milkan Watha*, and other poems,"
by Marc Antony Henderson, D.C.L. Cincinnati : *Tickell*
and *Grinne*. 1856.

NICOTINA.

After Tennyson's "Oriana."

    At a bal masqué in San Francisco a young lady appeared
attired to represent *Nicotine*. Her dress was made of Tobacco

leaves, her necklace was formed of cigars, and she carried a
fan and a parasol constructed of the weed.

My liver's out of order, oh !
     Nicotina !
A cloudy gloom doth o'er me flow,
     Nicotina !
When blossoms fall as white as snow,
I think of her of " Francisco,"
     Nicotina !
I wriggle in my bitter woe,
     Nicotina !

When the dark to light was growing,
     Nicotina !
And the cock left off a crowing,
     Nicotina !
Thin ones " oh "-ing, fat ones blowing,
All unto the ball were going,
     Nicotina !
I, too, went, to my o'erthrowing !
     Nicotina !

In the ball-room fill'd with light,
     Nicotina !
(Some were downstairs getting tight,
     Nicotina !)
While thine eyes entranced my sight,
Underneath the gay gaslight,
     Nicotina !
I engaged you ; you said " Right ! "
     Nicotina !

We danced in the whirling ball
     Nicotina !

She loved my mask 'mong them all,
> Nicotina !

She saw me slip, she heard me fall,
When out stepp'd a rival tall,
> Nicotina !

He kicked me hard, and made me bawl,
> Nicotina !

The villain dragg'd thee on one side,
> Nicotina !

The bitter beast, he went aside,
> Nicotina !

The darn'd brute, he glanced aside,
And took thee off, my love, my bride,
> Nicotina !

Thy dress, thy fan, and thee beside,
> Nicotina !

Oh ! narrow, narrow was the place,
> Nicotina !

I call'd out as a donkey brays,
> Nicotina !

Oh ! dreadful looks were dealt apace,
There was no room for dancing ways,
> Nicotina !

And flat I went upon my face !
> Nicotina !

They tried to smash me where I lay.
> Nicotina !

I couldn't rise and get away,
> Nicotina !

No more I thought to see the day,

They tried to smash me where I lay,
> Nicotina !
They nearly turn'd my dust to clay,
> Nicotina !

Oh ! breaking ribs, that would not break,
> Nicotina !
Oh ! damaged nose, so snub and meek,
> Nicotina !
She winketh, but she does not speak ;
I rub the chalk dust from my cheek,
> Nicotina !
And feel inclined away to sneak,
> Nicotina !

I cry, "my corns !" none hear my cries,
> Nicotina !
And, rueful, rub my blacken'd eyes,
> Nicotina !
My face is like to boneless size,
Up from my chin unto my eyes,
> Nicotina !
On thy programme my name it lies,
> Nicotina !

Oh ! cursed boot ! oh ! cursed blow,
> Nicotina !
I was not happy lying low,
> Nicotina !
All night my nose with blood did flow ;
A quart it bled, and more, I know,
> Nicotina !
A damaged man, away I go,
> Nicotina !

When my old pipe is lit by me
                    Nicotina !
I crawl about and think of thee,
                    Nicotina !
I do not dare to look at thee,
I fear *him*, tall as forest tree,
                    Nicotina !
I "cuss" him, and his pedigree.
                    Nicotina !

                         H. L.

O Darling Weed !

O DARLING weed ! my heart's delight,
Dear plant, the apple of my sight,
Thou hast a ray so warm and bright
I know no charm so exquisite
As puffing out thy smoke so white.
It puts all troublous thoughts to flight,
Sending dull spirits left and right,
While yielding joy by day and night.

This is a parody of a little poem by Alfred Tennyson,
published in 1833, but afterwards omitted from his works,
probably because of the ridicule it received from Lord
Lytton in "The New Timon" :—

O DARLING room, my heart's delight
Dear room, the apple of my sight,
With thy two couches soft and white,
There is no room so exquisite,
No little room so warm and bright,
Wherein to read, wherein to write.

          *   *   *   *

The Weed.

I come from vaunted root, and burn
  To many a merry sally;
I sparkle, and to ashes turn,
  Men's spirits worn to rally.

Thrice thirty ills that press folks down,
  I fumigate like midges;
In country, city, little town,
  My charm some care abridges.

Yon chattering Stiggins with a craze,
  In little sharps and trebles,
A hubbub makes in my dispraise—
  Demosthenes, *sans* pebbles.

Ay! chatter, with thy face of woe;
  With bile and anger quiver;
Thus Antis come and Antis go,
  But I'm smoked on for ever.

They go about, and fume and spout,
  Against Tobacco railing,
With here and there a lusty shout,
  And here and there a wailing.

I'm smoked on lawns and grassy plots,
  By sportsmen in the covers;
My cloud's blue as forget-me-nots
  That grow for happy lovers.

There is not under moon and stars,
  In this world's wildernesses,

A plant that care more stoutly bars,
  Or labour better blesses.

Behold my vapour curve and flow
  Tow'rds where the pure clouds quiver;
Let Antis come and Antis go—
  My smoke goes up for ever.

                                    R. C.

Cope's Tobacco Plant.   March, 1874.

———:o:———

SONG FROM THE MIKADO.

THE travellers who try in the spring,
                    Tra la!

  To sell their cigars by the case,
Must find it a difficult thing,
                    Tra la!
When the shopkeeper won't buy a thing,
                    Tra la!
  And kicks them right out of the place,
  And he kicks them all out of his place.
And that's what they mean when they say or they sing:
"Oh, bother the trade we are having this spring,"
                Tra la la la la la, tra la la la la,
                Tra la la la la la lah!

The following can scarcely be termed *parodies*, they are poems in praise of Tobacco written in the newly-revived but old-fashioned Ballade metre.

THE FRAGRANT PIPE.

["He who doth not smoke, either hath known no great sorrow or denieth himself the softest consolation."— BULWER-LYTTON.]

DENY yourselves this boon who choose,
Revile or scoff at us but we
Who know the helper you abuse
Can hear with calm philosophy.
Behold ! how in this cloud they flee,
Your small vexations of a day—
The mountain-molehills that you see—
   A fragrant pipe drives care away.

The neediest servant of the Muse
Asks not your aid to set him free,
Though editors his rhymes refuse,
This is the friend of poverty.
This is the comforter that he
Shall turn to for his surest stay,
Though out at elbow, worn at knee,
   A fragrant pipe drives care away.

For by this aid fresh evils lose
Their sharpest sting, their worst degree ;
Old cares and sorrows it subdues
Into a dreamy memory.

And still while on our shelves may be
One well-browned meerschaum, briar or clay,
We laugh at the relentless three,
    A fragrant pipe drives care away.

ENVOI.

King James ! with all respect to thee,
Tobacco held the surest sway,
Despite thy "counterblast's decree,"
    A fragrant pipe drives care away.

From *The Cigar and Tobacco World.*   April 15, 1889.

BALLADE OF THE BEST PIPE.

I HEAR you fervently extol
    The virtues of your ancient clay,
As black as any piece of coal.
To me it smells of rank decay
And bones of people passed away,—
    A smell I never could admire.
    With all respect to you I say,
Give me a finely seasoned briar.

Poor Jones, whose judgment as a whole
    Is faultless, has been led astray
To nurse a costly meerschaum bowl.
Well, let him nurse it as he may,
I hardly think he'll find it pay.
    Before the colour gets much higher,
    He'll drop it on the grate some day.
Give me a finely seasoned brier.

The heathen Turk of Istamboul,
 In Oriental turban gay,
Delights his unregenerate soul
With hookahs, bubbling in a way
To fill a Christian with dismay,
 And wake the old Crusading fire.
 May no such pipe be mine I pray !
Give me a finely seasoned brier

ENVOY.

Clay, meerschaum, hookah, what are they
 That I should view them with desire?
I'll sing, till all my hair is grey,
 Give me a finely seasoned brier.

The University News Sheet. St. Andrews, N. B.
 March 3, 1886.

THE BALLADE OF TOBACCO.

WHEN verdant youth sees life afar,
 And first sets out wild oats to sow,
He puffs a stiff and stark cigar,
 And quaffs champagne of Mumm & Co.
 He likes not smoking yet ; but though
Tobacco makes him sick indeed,
 Cigars and wine he can't forego :—
A slave is each man to the weed.

In time his tastes more dainty are,
 And delicate. Become a beau,
From out the country of the Czar
 He brings his cigarettes, and lo !
 He sips the vintage of Bordeaux.

Thus keener relish shall succeed
   The baser liking we outgrow :—
A slave is each man to the weed.

When age and his own lucky star
   To him perfected wisdom show,
The schooner glides across the bar,
   And beer for him shall freely flow,
   A pipe with genial warmth shall glow ;
To which he turns in direst need,
   To seek in smoke surcease of woe :—
A slave is each man to the weed.

ENVOI.

Smokers ! who doubt or con or pro,
   And ye who dare to drink, take heed !
And see in smoke a friendly foe : —
   A slave is each man to the weed.

BRANDER MATTHEWS.

From Mr. Gleeson White's collection of *Ballades and Rondeaus.* London, Walter Scott, 1887.

——

IN A CLOUD OF SMOKE.

A Rondel.

IN a cloud of smoke when the lights are low
I half forget that I'm nearly " broke,"
And my cares and my sorrows they seem to go
    In a cloud of smoke.

Ah, yes! 'tis a mystical " Basingstoke,"*
That guides my thoughts to a saner flow
So a fig to the Anti-Tobacco folk!

Her tongue has no "measured beat and slow ; "
She says that in fumes narcotic I soak ;
But her withering scorn seems to softer grow
                In a cloud of smoke.
From *Judy.*   April 18, 1888.

With Pipe and Book.

With Pipe and Book at close of day,
O! what is sweeter, mortal, say?
It matters not what book on knee,
Old Izaak or the Odyssey,
It matters not meerschaum or clay.

And though our eyes will dream astray,
And lips forget to sue or sway,
It is " enough to merely *Be*,"
              With Pipe and Book.

What though our modern skies be grey,
As bards aver, I will not pray
For " soothing death " to " succour " me,
But ask thus much, O! Fate, of thee,
A little longer yet to stay
              With Pipe and Book.

From *Volumes in Folio.* By Richard Le Gallienne,
author of " My Ladies' Sonnets," etc.   London, Elkin
Matthews, Vigo Street, W. 1889.
A dainty little Volume of Bookish Verses.

---

* An allusion to a phrase in *Ruddigore.*

Lines on an Empty Tobacco-pouch.

I, WHO was brisk and R T once,
Am C D now ; become a dunce.
If U the reason would descry,
I'll very quickly tell U Y.

I ne'er indulged in sad I—OOO !
When smoke was curling round my N—OOO ;
But I am falling 2 D K,
Who could X L, no distant day.

I lack not T, or O D V,
But B 4 long my want U'll C :
My pouch is M T ; so, indeed,
I N V men with lots of weed.

I C U feel an interest
In what your poet would request ;
There 4 I ask U 2 X QQQ
The plaint of my dejected M UUU.

I C U R the smoker's friend ;
Send me some weed B 4 my end !
This craving I would fain ap PPP,
And smoke my pipe "O K" at EEE.

Declare I lived and died in peace,
If U should hear of my D CCC.
Erect an F-I-G of me,
And write this in my L-E-G.

Here lies a man of Letters, C,
Who shunned X S ; and yet was E

Merry and YYY ; a busy B,
Who never made an N M E.

From *Cope's Tobacco Plant.*   November 1871.

———:0:———

THE SMOKER'S ALPHABET.

A   was an Anti-Tobacconist moke,
B   was the 'Bacca his neighbours *would* smoke,
C   was the Counsel he forced on the world,
D   was Derision, that at him was hurled.
E   more Enlightened, would chuckle and say,
F   "Fill your pipes, and puff nonsense away."
G   was a Guardsman, who lit a cigar ;
H   was the health that it never could mar.
I   was an Irishman witty and gay,
J   was the Joy that his pipe gave each day.
K   was the Keel of the vessel that bore
L   Lots of the "Weed" from Columbia's shore.
M   was the Mariner, chewing a quid,
N   was a Noodle, who vowed "If he did,
O   "Only 'Orrible qualms would arise."
P   was the Punch that he got 'twixt his eyes,
Q   with the Quid ; he turned sickly and wan,
R   was the "Robert" who made him "move on."
S   was the Snuff, pungent, fragrant, and light,
T   the Torment of Headache cured by it quite.
U   the plant Universal, that is still
V   the Victor over full many an ill.
W   the Wealth, that its growers may hoard,
X   is a Xebeck, with tobacco on board.
Y   was a Yankee, who offered cheroots,
Z   was a Zealot, who said "Fit for brutes !"
&   the Yankee replied,"Brutes don't talk,or wear boots."

The Smoker's Philosophy.

Oh! 'tis very pleasant ; thus to sit and smoke
Makes a peer of peasant, of sad life a joke ;
What are cares and troubles, what are hopes and fears?
Scarce so many bubbles—in a hundred years.

What your weight or worth then, who the deuce will care?
What you did on earth then, who on earth you were?
Who the dickens nursed you? Who for you shed tears?
Who shed none, but cursed you—in a hundred years?

'Twill be all the same lad if with drum and fife
You've enjoyed a game lad, or a quiet life,
Used a spade or sabre, fed your friends or steers ;
You'll have ceased from labour—in a hundred years.

Still there will be flowers lad, some more fruit be ripe ;
True 'twill not be ours lad ; smoke another pipe,
Then off ourselves to bed take ; pretty little dears,
I warrant we've no headache—in a hundred years

J. A. Colwyn.   1873.

THE
Works of WALTER HAMILTON.

~~~~~~~~~~~~~~~~~~~~~~~~~~~

THE
POETS LAUREATE
OF ENGLAND:

BEING

A History of the Office of Poet Laureate, Biographical Notices of its Holders, and a Collection of the Satires, Epigrams, and Lampoons directed against them.

~~~~~~~~~~~~~~~~~~~~~~~~~~~~~~~~

OPINIONS OF THE PRESS.

"The author of this amusing volume has spared no pains to make it as complete as possible, and it is a good instance of the progress that we have made of late years in the production of literary history. Mr. Hamilton's pages will not only be found useful for purposes of reference, but extremely entertaining to an idle reader." "The Athenæum." January 18, 1879.

"Recommendation can scarcely be necessary to secure proper attention for 'The Poets Laureate of England,' by Walter Hamilton, inasmuch as the very title is pretty sure to attract notice and pique curiosity. It may be worth while, however, to remark at once that, what with the care, diligence, and judgment which have apparently been brought to bear upon the whole composition of the book the public have a chance of obtaining a volume so interesting, so trustworthy, so instructive, and so manageable, that they have no small reason to thank the author for his trouble. In his preface and introduction he displays no little learning and research, and brings before his readers information touching matters in which they should be glad to be instructed."—"Illustrated London News." Feb., 15, 1879.

REEVES & TURNER, 196, STRAND, LONDON.

History of every kind of Parody and Burlesque, British and American, in a form admitting of easy reference, and particularly suitable for Public Entertainments, Penny Readings, and Comic Recitations.

The following is a list of Contents of the Collection so far as it has been completed at the present time.

<table>
<tr><td>William Shakespeare</td><td>Mrs. Hemans.</td></tr>
<tr><td>Alfred, Lord Tennyson</td><td>Robert Southey.</td></tr>
<tr><td>Henry W. Longfellow</td><td>The Anti-Jacobin.</td></tr>
<tr><td>Thomas Hood.</td><td>Lord Byron.</td></tr>
<tr><td>Edgar Allan Poe.</td><td>Thomas Moore.</td></tr>
<tr><td>John Milton.</td><td>Sentimental Songs.</td></tr>
<tr><td>John Dryden.</td><td>Naval and Military Songs.</td></tr>
<tr><td>Dr. Isaac Watts.</td><td>"The Bilious Beadle"</td></tr>
<tr><td>Miss Taylor's "My Mother."</td><td>Patriotic Songs.</td></tr>
<tr><td>"Not a Drum was Heard."</td><td>Songs by W. S. Gilbert.</td></tr>
<tr><td>Bret Harte.</td><td>English Songs and Ballads.</td></tr>
<tr><td>Matthew Arnold.</td><td>Charles Mackay's Songs.</td></tr>
<tr><td>Oliver Goldsmith.</td><td>R. B. Sheridan's Songs.</td></tr>
<tr><td>Thomas Campbell.</td><td>Barry Cornwall's Songs.</td></tr>
<tr><td>Robert Burns.</td><td>(B. W. Proctor).</td></tr>
<tr><td>Sir Walter Scott.</td><td>Scotch, Irish, and Welsh Songs.</td></tr>
<tr><td>Scotch Songs.</td><td>Mrs. Norton's Poems.</td></tr>
<tr><td>Charles Kingsley.</td><td>Gray's "Elegy," & other Poems.</td></tr>
</table>

Cowper's "John Gilpin" and other Poems.

William Wordsworth's Poems.

Coleridge's "Ancient Mariner" and "Christabel."

M. G Lewis's "Alonzo the Brave," and Leigh Hunt.

Lord Macaulay's Poems.

W. M. Praed's Poems, "Good Night to the Season," etc., "The Devil's Walk," "My name is Norval," "Pity the Sorrows of a Poor Old Man," and "Wanted, a Governess."

W. M. Thackeray, Lord Lytton, P. B. Shelley, and Mrs. E. B. Browning's Poems.

Parodies of American Poetry, "Maud Muller," "Kate Ketchem," "Barbara Fritchie," "Sheridan's Ride."

American National and Patriotic Poems.

Oliver Wendell Holmes, Col. John Hay, Walt Whitman, J. R. Lowell, and R. W. Emerson.

The Ingoldsby Legends, By R. H. Barham.

Joseph Addison, W. Collins, and Samuel Rogers.

Algernon C. Swinburne.

George R. Sims.

Robert Browning, F. Locker-Lampson, and D. G. Rossetti.

W. Morris, Oscar Wilde, and Martin F. Tupper.

Nursery Rhymes.

Parodies in Praise of Tobacco.

John Dryden and Alexander Pope.   [Others will follow.